WHAT LIES IN THE DARK

CM THOMPSON

BLOODHOUND
— BOOKS —

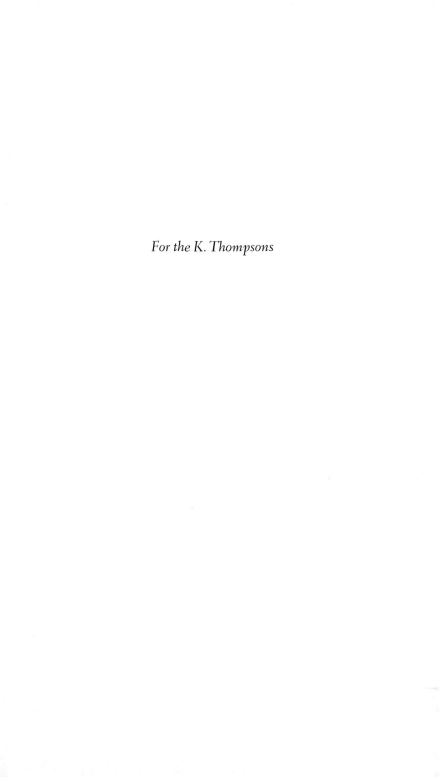

For the K. Thompsons

CHAPTER ONE

A nita Gardner is eight years old and she is afraid. It is a terrible thing to be eight and so afraid. She is afraid of spiders and their webs. She is afraid of the thing that lives under the bed. Mummy says it doesn't exist, but she knows it does. She can hear it moving in the darkness, scratching and growling, just waiting for the right moment to pounce. Anita is afraid of the big boys at school, the ones who are already ten and so much bigger than her. She has seen them picking on Mary Taylor. Anita spends her break times hiding in corners of the playground, hoping that they don't come for her. Anita is afraid of maths tests and the big girls' homework her sister brings home. Anita is afraid of dogs, and wasps, and spiders. She is afraid of the forest that she is walking through right now. She doesn't usually walk this way but she needed to go in the opposite direction to the big boys. Even though that means she now must walk along the edge of the forest on her own, to get home.

Anita is too afraid to cry, she really wants to but she can't. Around her she can hear the sound of twigs breaking, strange shrieks and some animal closing in. A wasp buzzes past scaring her so badly she breaks into a run, her pudgy legs moving as fast as her little body can go, not quite realising what direction she is running in, just wanting to get home. Faster and faster she runs, her heart beating so loudly she can no longer hear the monsters.

Of course she is going to trip, no one can run in a forest when they have strayed from the path. There are always roots and branches for a foot to trip on and when she finally falls, she lies shaking, not realising that her leg is bleeding or that she has torn her school skirt. If she makes it home her mother is going to be so angry but she is not thinking about that right now, she is not thinking at all. She is just lying in the dirt there, waiting for the monsters, the ogres, to leap out of the woods their claws reaching out to grab her, their mouths snarling in anticipation.

Nothing moves, she holds her breath, warm tears still pouring down her chubby cheeks. Her heart pounds, thudding in her ears, waiting for the grab on her legs, hands, shoulders. For jaws to chomp down hard on her flesh. Slowly but heroically she will eventually summon enough courage to stand up and limp unsteadily home. In a few years' time she will even look back on this and laugh at her childish ways, never again will she fear the woods or the monsters or the dark. She will never ever know that she fell onto the grave of Victim Number Eight.

Anita Gardner knew Victim Number Eight. Anita knew her as a very nice lady called Joanna Reagan. Earlier this year Joanna started her teacher training at Anita's school. Anita really likes that pretty lady who smiles at everything. Anita has made Miss Reagan a very nice picture and is waiting eagerly to give it to her. No one knows yet that Joanna is missing. The school has presumed that Joanna has given up and gone home, they are disappointed that she didn't tell them she was leaving but it happens all the time. Her family at home thinks she is too busy to contact them. They haven't heard from her since Easter and are starting to worry. "This isn't like her," her mother mutters. It will be a good few weeks before Joanna is reported missing, before her mother will appeal in the local newspapers for Joanna just to contact her, *no matter what has happened, please just come home.* It will be two years before people realise that there is a serial killer on the loose, and Joanna will always be missing, never found.

They call the occupant of that house, Old Man Krill or The Krill. It is a house close to a park and every day shrill voices speculate on its owner, the local bogeyman. The Krill sits by the door waiting for a child to wander into the back garden and then it's lunchtime! This would be acted out; the storyteller grabbing a foolish listener who got too close, always good for a scream or two. The adults talk about this house too, in more hushed voices and serious tones.

"Don't go near that house, sweetie, a bad bad man lives in that house. I want you to promise never to go near that house," is the cliché on every mother's lips.

"They say Old Krill found his girlfriend with another man and he chopped them both into little pieces and then he ate them! Not even the cops will go near that place."

Rumours are spreading, everyone talks of Old Krill, they know so many different stories; it is a drug den, a brothel which receives no clients, an abortionist clinic for Daddy's little secret. In tamer stories, it houses a greasy geek intent on world domination, a meth lab or sometimes a sarcastic voice talks of an old lady with nine cats.

"I dare you to ... push the doorbell on The Krill's place."

"I don't want to."

"What are you? Chicken? Cluck cluck cluck."

"Does little chicken want his mummy?"

Joanna Reagan's mother is constantly crying on television and pleading for her daughter to come home. The Christmas after Joanna disappeared is too painful to even mention. Her mother has answered the phone to what seems like a million well-wishers, pranksters and relatives. Joanna still has not come home. Joanna's younger sister has pierced her nose, dyed her hair six different colours and had nine temper tantrums on the stairs, in small desperate attempts to make her mother notice her. None of the relatives, well-wishers or reporters ever ask about her whilst Joanna is idolised and memorialised. Even Joanna's room, the bigger one, the one which her sister had been promised when Joanna left for university, remains a shrine to Joanna.

Joanna is now just a memory. Her body is not recognisable as Joanna anymore, even the number 8 so painstakingly carved into her right hand has decayed away. After a year only her mother is still hopeful that she will come home.

Whilst rumours of Joanna Reagan grow cold, The Krill rumours become more sinister and creepy, truly in all areas he is now the spider waiting in the dark.

CHAPTER TWO

I t's going to be an unusually nice spring day. Fran Lizzie is lying in a near perfect spot. She is positioned in front of a fence, spread out on luscious green grass, which is lightly tickling her unblemished skin. Fran Lizzie is a pretty girl, very photogenic. She is dressed in a blue shirt with denim jeans with splashes of red. She is staring up at a beautiful clear blue sky, as birds chirp in tune with the burbling and gurgling of a river. Nature is happily beginning the day with no respect for the dead.

Fran Lizzie would have been quite comfortable, if her leg had not been trapped on the merciless iron fence, firmly wedged between the bars, giving her fallen body a slightly twisted effect. But that is nothing, a sting compared to the deep gouge that is spread across her neck, still staining the ground with drips of red. She has been alone for a while, unnoticed, no one really pays attention around here anymore. Fran Lizzie's sightless eyes cannot see the sun rise nor will she hear the first scream of the new day.

A man passes, walking his dog, at first seeing just a blur of a girl, he is not really looking, doesn't stop to think how a girl could have got over that iron fence. He doesn't want to know, doesn't want to be involved with broken rules. His dog strains at the lead, whining. He tries to pull the dog forward, anxious to go home and get ready for work. The dog is stubborn, refusing to move as he turns to get a tighter grip on the leash and perhaps share an embarrassed look with the girl on the grass. He finally looks then he loosens his grip, his arms falling limp as blood gushes toward his heart. As he catches a better view of the mutilated lady lying in the lake of red.

"What the fuck..." he whispers.

The police arrive, closely followed by an unnecessary ambulance. Their first task is to get over the iron fence, a fence designed to keep people out, a fence that had been resurrected to stop anyone from playing in the dirty river. The key to the iron gate cannot be located, so the first responders have no choice but to climb over the fence, trying so hard not to contaminate the crime scene, careful not to step into the red pond. But hoping, despite everything for a sign of life.

She is photographed from every angle, hundreds of digital photographs documenting her final violation. Particular attention is paid to the crude cuts in her hand. Then Jane Doe is officially pronounced dead and cautiously removed. The crime scene investigators start the long meticulous task of clearing the scene, sealing nine shrivelled condoms, twelve cigarette butts and six crushed beer cans carefully into paper bags to be sent to the backlogged lab. They spend hours sweating into their plastic protective suits as the small crowd of onlookers grows. Working patiently, ignoring the catcalls and photographs of the media, as the stench of the algae river wafts by, while flies nosedive around their heads. The area has never looked cleaner when they finish, if you can ignore the pool of the congealed blood, soon to be washed away.

The word spread faster than blood, while the investigators worked, the word spread through every community, twisting in shape and rumour that a body ... no, two bodies! Have been found, mutilated! Their eyes missing! High schools are filling with hushed whispers, they have found a young woman, no, man! Suspicions and worries are cast on every absent student, small children are in tears, provoked by cruel lies, ringing home frantically just to check ... mobiles ring and ring and ring.

Someone has even tried phoning Fran Lizzie, who cannot answer her phone right now. Even though she is late for work, two hours and ten minutes late and her boss is counting. Fran Lizzie's phone briefly rang, until the last of Fran Lizzie's battery died, buried behind the dissolving mints in Fran Lizzie's sinking purse. The purse is submerged in the contaminated river water, caught on a rusty shopping trolley, downstream from where the officers are dragging. He threw it in the river just for fun, after taking a different trophy. He will later laugh to himself as he sits, listening to people complain about what the hell they might have caught at the riverbank.

Detective Sergeant Aaron Fletcher and his senior partner, Bullface, have been assigned to this case. Victoria Bullrush, Victoria never Vicky 'Don't Call Me Bullface' Bullrush. Bullface is the kind of cop who could never work under cover. Everything about her just squeals cop, her stance, her clothing and her attitude. Everything down to the permanently embedded frown. In her twenty years of service she has played by every rule and will tolerate no breaking or bending of the law. Even her husband will carefully obey speed limits when she is in the car.

Fletcher and Bullface are on the wrong side of that iron fence where Fran Lizzie was found, gazing down on the cleared grass.

"She was killed here, facing the fence. Most of the spatter is on the grass. Then she was thrown over the fence, as yet no ID. I have a team dragging the river at the moment, Michaels is going through *Missings* ... body has no defensive wounds, no sign of sexual assault."

Bullface looks down at the splattered drops of blood. She, Jane Doe, had been facing the river, he was behind her, probably pointing to something across the river, *Look what's that?* There would be minimal blood splatter on him, mostly likely on his sleeve, staining as he drew the knife across her throat. Possibly they might find his clothing fibres on the back of Jane Doe's clothes ... possibly. It is something to start with. She gazes down on the impression Jane Doe had left on the grass, Jane Doe had been killed and then discarded with little regard. It was dubious that this had been a personal kill. Bullface surveys the once quiet street, only a few reporters remain now, photographing whatever looks shocking, still held at bay by scintillating yellow police tape. Jane Doe's death will not make global or even national news just yet. The images of the empty street, of the iron fence and its enclosed darkness, contrasting against the sharp yellow tape will just make local news. The images will be slapped on to the third page of tomorrow's newspaper alongside a small head shot of what used to be Fran Lizzie Taylor.

There are no houses nearby, this street is just an isolated shortcut home for many anonymous people. Fletcher, in a mad moment of twisted philosophy, wonders if a girl screams in the middle of the street and no one is around to hear it, how do we know she screamed? The bubble is beginning to boil in the pit of his stomach, the dark dried stain amalgamating in his head.

Bullface is thinking more professionally. Fran Lizzie was probably very light, like a doll, says an unwanted thought. Skimpy thing, lack of defensive wounds means that she probably didn't put up much of a fight, might not even have known what was happening. An easy kill in other words. The bastard must have been very strong, strong enough to lift her over a five foot fence. Tall, dark, strong and handsome, all the traits of a bastard. It could have been two bastards, that would have made the throwing easier, but considering the lack of sexual assault, lack of defensive wounds, the way Fran Lizzie's foot had been caught on the fence, suggesting he hadn't quite made the toss. These things all said that there was just one. The unwanted questions begin to pile in her mind. Did he choose a girl he knew he could lift? This site felt too planned to be accidental. He must know this area well, must have planned this ... had he planned it to be her? Did she mean something to him? The way she had been discarded suggested not, but there was still a possibility. Why leave her here? She was found so easily, like he was challenging them, look at me, look at me, you can't catch me... an unwelcome shiver runs down Bullface's spine. A planned dumpsite, a planned open kill, a kill that seems too planned to be a first kill. A rational killer who knows what he is doing. Then there were also the crude cuts to consider. The killer must have been very confident to take the time to make those, confident no one would disturb and then there was what he had carved ... her thoughts are interrupted by two triumphant shouts, echoing across the muddy water, one part of the team eagerly pulls out a briefcase, the other part of the team a women's purse, both stolen both oozing grunge, neither actually belonging to Fran Lizzie.

Today's thirtieth caller will discover that their flatmate is dead. It is one in a sea of calls echoing that a girlfriend, a boyfriend, a sister, a brother, cannot be found and wasn't answering their phone. One of many echoes stating that my neighbour, friend, lover did not come home last night. As news of a body spreads, people begin to notice that someone is missing, someone isn't there. The survivors are jamming the phone lines, trying to reach out with a desperate plea, please don't be them ... *If I tell you what s/he looks like, then please tell me it's not them, please* ... It is her, Fran Lizzie Taylor lying in the morgue with the number 22 cut into her left hand.

Fran Lizzie had been an ordinary twenty-two-year-old woman, living in a shared apartment. Monday to Friday she worked as a sales assistant. Friday nights she went a little wild to break up the monotony of the week. On Saturdays she would sleep till noon, only sometimes alone and then spend the rest of the day either shopping or visiting spas. On Sundays she would do all the little stupid jobs like the ironing or the washing and mostly relax. She was planning her summer holiday in detail fantasising about the sun, sand and sangria. Holiday brochures were everywhere in her flat, along with boxes of unworn shoes and coloured scarves. Fran Lizzie liked her life, liked her new boyfriend, Steve, who might just have been the one. Fran Lizzie liked it all, even her flat felt smiley and happy.

Bullface and Fletcher are now standing in the mess that was Fran Lizzie's living room, with the intention of interviewing her sobbing flatmate. Fletcher who specialises in interviewing techniques, prides himself on being able to talk to anyone even the scummiest of scum. But he always feels a little helpless when faced with a sobbing young woman, this woman is no exception.

"She … she … waaaaaaah … she…" More mascara trickles down her stained cheeks.

"Take a deep breath," Fletcher advises as compassionately as he can. They have been trying for ten minutes now to find out where Fran Lizzie had gone last night and his patience is wearing a little thin.

"She … she … arrgggh."

Fletcher patiently passes her a fresh tissue, while Bullface, who has little patience, continues her visual inspection of the living room, scanning the vast pile of scattered DVDs, looking for a sign that Fran or her flatmate were not as girly as they appeared. All she can see are chick-flicks, chick-flicks and more chick-flicks. Smiling happy actors stare out of abandoned DVD cases mocking Bullface's thoughts. Even the walls of the living room are painted a soothing light pink. There seems little possibility that Fran or her flatmate are moonlighting as dominatrix or anything even remotely dark. The room contains no explanation of why Fran had been picked to die.

"She … waaas going to … mughgo hgggr bddoosfid." The flatmate tries again, choking in the folds of her nineteenth fresh tissue.

"I am sorry, what was that?"

"Meeet … hsffji frhg."

"She was going to meet who?" Fletcher is met with a fresh wail of tears. This is going to take a while, a long while. His colleagues are not having much more luck either. Extra volunteer staff have been brought in to deal with the barrage of phone calls, as exaggerated rumours are still spreading. Officers have been sent around nearby streets to interview potential eyewitnesses. No one saw or heard anything strange last night. Well that's not true, several screams had been heard, it was a typical drunk Friday night. Fran Lizzie had been found thirty minutes away from a very popular pub. She had been last seen leaving that pub, after meeting one of her workmates for a drink. Her flatmate was supposed to go with her but after a bad argument with her boyfriend, she decided to stay at home, something she would regret for the rest of her life. Something Fran Lizzie regretted for the last few moments of her life.

No one had seen anything out of the ordinary, Fran Lizzie had three vodka and cranberry juices before leaving. Her workmate would say later that she was happy, laughing over the rudest customer of that day, talking eagerly of her planned holiday to Ibiza. She had left the pub alone. The workmate had been busy chatting up a crush. No one had noticed anything suspicious or anyone following her.

The last day of Fran Lizzie's life had just been like any other day.

Bullface and Fletcher left the flatmate sobbing and returned to the office to spend the last two hours of their shift writing up statements and reports, conferring with their colleagues over the total lack of evidence. Bullface and Fletcher had been assigned to this case, two other detective constables to a rape. Tomorrow will bring more interviews, more reports and the single fading hope that this is a one off.

Why 22? What significance did it have? They briefly consider the possibilities. Fran Lizzie was twenty-two and, ironically, twenty-two days. There was a possibility that her killer knew that. But then, Fletcher decides, her killer probably didn't know her, nothing about this murder has suggested it is a personal hate kill. Bullface backs him up here, the way Fran Lizzie was so carelessly thrown over a fence, as if she meant nothing to the assailant. It was too cold, too calculating to be the work of someone who had known her.

Maybe only time will reveal this secret connection, maybe it was the start of some kind of code (Bullface personally thinks that this is a stupid suggestion). The cuts had been inflicted post mortem so it was extremely unlikely Fran Lizzie had inflicted them herself for whatever reason. It made Bullface remember a certain street crazy who regularly carved words into himself, etching random names, a shopping list and an illegible list. Come to think of it, Bullface hadn't seen him around lately. She had never asked him why, it seemed to her an idiotic question to ask but maybe next time she sees him, if she sees him again. They all work on the premise that if you take the time to permanently carve something into skin, then it has to mean something, even if no one else understands the meaning. The number on Fran Lizzie has to mean something, anything but the most logical explanation, the one that they are all praying, hoping isn't true, that this does not mean that she is victim number 22. That there are twenty-one others out there, somewhere, screaming silently in the dark and dirt.

The pubs are quiet tonight, unusually quiet for a Saturday night. Not many women want to risk going out, especially not alone. Next week they will forget and the pubs will be filled again, but not tonight. Tonight people are mourning a girl most of them have never met and now never will. Perhaps people are paranoid thinking that he might strike again tonight. Every smooth-tongued man could be him, every drink could be spiked. Tonight, he could be here out to get another unsuspecting victim. Everywhere the atmosphere is tense, though ironically, the pubs are the safest place to be.

The conversations are all about him, so many hushed whispers as every stranger, every loner is carefully scrutinised. Inevitably, "Maybe it was The Krill," is one joke made by several different groups, a joke always met with nervous laughter, no one wanting to acknowledge the dark truth lying behind the joke. It could be The Krill. No one is even sure of what The Krill looks like. Here tonight, and tomorrow night perhaps even for the rest of the year, people are thinking carelessly, jumping straight to conclusions and that is always dangerous. This isn't the first murder that this city has seen, not even the first this year, but the fact that it is a young girl, killed with no obvious motive. The fact that the news has covered it so mysteriously: confirming the mutilation but not giving any juicy details has sent the city into motion. Several super-sleuths are already blaming her boyfriend, romanticising the idea of a torrid affair, maybe with her boss, which had been fatally discovered. Not knowing that Fran Lizzie's boss is actually a happily married sixty-year-old woman.

Stella is still working tonight, she has heard about the murder but she doesn't really care. Stella isn't going to lose forty, sixty quid over some girl. Stupid bint probably deserved it anyway. Stella hoists her short neon skirt even higher, revealing even more tantalising thigh. The lack of girls out tonight is going to work to her benefit anyway. Might even make eighty tonight.

The sword squelches through the green flesh, pixels of blood washing across the screen before dramatically fading as the orc falls to the ground. Another one bites the dust. Kain, even after two hundred orcs is still thirsty for more, craving that teeny rush of power derived from a kill. The power Kain so rarely feels in real life, the secret thrill of just being better than everyone else at something drives Kain to continue. It isn't as if there was anything better to do right now, not just yet.

Slice, slash, and squelch. Next!

Kain inhales another lungful of smoke, heightening the heady rush of orc demise, maybe next it should be a dragon demise. Every so often just checking, making sure there is no chance. No, but you have to be sure, just have to check ... no definitely not, safe for now...

Fran Lizzie's flatmate has finally stopped wailing. She is staring blankly at Fran Lizzie's bedroom door, just waiting for Fran Lizzie to get up. Fran's jacket is still draped across the kitchen chair. Her dirty dishes from last night's dinner still lie in the sink, three messages from Steve are bleeping on the answer machine. The whole flat seems to be waiting for Fran to come home. To step through that door, because everything is just fine and everything is OK and Fran will be here, any minute now, any minute now ... now ... now. Fran Lizzie's flatmate just doesn't know what else to do, so she is sitting here, waiting ... waiting. Tomorrow Fran Lizzie's mother will be here and there will be more tears and her flatmate will finally realise. But for now she is just waiting and waiting, staring numbly at the closed door.

Brandi is listening to her mother bragging on and on about the nice young man her sister is seeing, a bright young man who just happens to earn lots of money doing some computer nonsense. Her mother will never understand the internet industry, always arguing that it is for people who have too much time on their hands ... but those who are making their fortunes from such an industry, *Well hello, Mister, and do have some tea.*

Brandi can't stand listening to her mother's insistent "You could also find such a man if you tried, maybe if you straightened your hair and wore that dress I got you for

Christmas." The offending unworn dress that Brandi had decided made her look like a thirty-something has-been hooker.

Brandi sometimes wondered what her mother actually wanted from her. Why torture her every week with, "You could be like your sister if only you would…" What exactly did her mother want? Brandi had a goodish job, she didn't want for anything (well maybe those boots she had seen recently, so sexily centred in the shop's window). But that just wasn't good enough for Brandi's mother, oh no. She had to be sleeping with the next nerdy millionaire and buying diamonds like candy. The resentment is enough to make Brandi want to drink until sunrise because Brandi knows, her mother knows, her sister also knows that Brandi will never be good enough, she will never date the right man, or wear the right clothes, never do anything quite right. The next-door neighbour and the milkman also probably knows. So why does her mother do this to her? Why continue to torture her every week with nagging whines?

Brandi decides it is simply because her mother is Satan reincarnated.

Fletcher is cooking, it is what he does, particularly when he is stressed or worried. He doesn't do decorating or cars, the sad kitchen will attest to that. He is standing in a kitchen that is desperately in need of a paint job, the grease-stained walls need to be re-tiled and while we are on the subject, his car needs a wash and a vacuum, and Mrs Claire Fletcher would be very happy if Fletcher would just clean out the empty crisp packets. He won't, not while there is still room for his feet.

Tonight Fletcher has finally decided he is in the mood for chilli. The chilli recipe his mother had written down was neat and precise. She has even added little explanations to each ingredient, explaining why the cumin/chilli/paprika need to be added, to flavour the meat and dull the harshness of the red chilli powder. After careful deliberation Fletcher decides that Chinese five spice and mixed herbs are just as good. He pokes around the overflowing cupboard for kidney beans, Claire had promised to buy some and they are in there, behind the tins of mixed vegetables. But Fletcher cannot immediately see them, which means they are not there. Giving up, he decides that baked beans are just as good and throws those in instead. Stirring the concoction briefly, he thinks the chilli is looking pretty damn fine, get a whiff of that, lads! His stomach is rumbling in anticipation.

Fletcher then chops the peppers, concentrating every brain cell on not cutting his fingers, just focusing on slicing through the thick green flesh of the pepper, forgetting again to remove the pepper seeds. Trying to think only of the food and not the female, chop, now lying, chop chop, dead on the cold glass chopping board, chop chop chop, every violated piece being probed, chop chop, by the doctor's scalpel. Examined then thrown to boil. Chop chop, trying to focus on chopping the wretched peppers and not those tiresome questions, chop chop, why no defence wounds? Chop chop chop! Why didn't she struggle? Chop! Chop! Why 22? Chop! Why aren't there any kidney beans? Claire had promised, chop chop chop! She had promised to come straight home! Chop! Cho– the peppers have been slaughtered, the burning pan is making protesting fizzles but Fletcher is no longer hungry.

CHAPTER THREE

F our months have passed, Fran Lizzie Taylor and her secrets are long buried and her tombstone is still covered with flowers. Her smiling photo has haunted the city's television screens for long enough and has been replaced by someone more alive. People have calmed down, there doesn't appear to be any more danger. Fran is no longer even whispered about, even Fran Lizzie's part of the flat has been emptied by one of her brothers, with most of her possessions going to charity. The magazines advertising fun in the sun were recycled and the holiday to Ibiza completely forgotten. Despite this, Fran Lizzie's flatmate is still waiting for Fran to come home.

No one has been charged for Fran Lizzie's murder yet. Fran Lizzie's boyfriend, Steve, was investigated and even his mother will still regard him with suspicion for a while, but Bullface, to her disappointment, has proved him to be innocent. Not that Steve really cares, he has lost the one person he was living for, for now anyway. Fletcher and Bullface still wait patiently for the DNA results to be returned. Hoping for some kind of match to anyone, doesn't really matter who, just so this would be an easy open and shut case. Anything that might indicate that 22 was just an attempt to baffle them away from a personal kill. Someone out there must have disliked Fran Lizzie for a reason, there must be something to make this easier but they know the truth, Steve is innocent, Fran's family and flatmate who all have been DNA tested will also be innocent. Maybe something will be on her clothes or the cigarettes or the briefcase, a little speck of his DNA. The random objects might not be random, there is always a chance. Maybe, but the chances are low. They have got nowhere with the carved number. While Fletcher thinks it might be a code or something along those lines, Bullface believes it means Fran Lizzie is the twenty-second victim and that they should be looking for others. It just sounds so unlikely, how could there be others? So many others, surely someone would have noticed something ... she wants to start searching but she doesn't know where to start. Bullface has realised that she is just waiting for the next murder, knowing there will be another one, while Fletcher remains a little more optimistic. To him, this could still be a one-off well-disguised murder of passion. They are also investigating several other cases, which are looking a little more promising. That is not a comfort to Fran Lizzie's mother, Jennifer Taylor who still phones every week wanting to hear of progress, always hanging up angry and disappointed.

Marie Eine is unremarkable. Marie is a little like Joanna Reagan, patient, still ... skeletonised. Marie does not have a family wondering where she is, no one really noticed when she disappeared. No one has noticed her in all the years she has been lying here. Marie has been covered in leaves, eaten by bugs, pulled apart and scattered by animals, but she is still waiting for someone to realise that she is here. She has been waiting even longer than Joanna.

This morning, with great excitement, a child will pick up

her skull and proudly show it to horrified parents. Police will be called, another investigation will start. Unfortunately Marie Eine won't be identified to the rest of the world, she is Jane Doe 217, her bones will forever remain unclaimed. Some little bone fragments will still remain here, waiting, in this part of the forest. One or two of her teeth have been trodden further into the dirt by unsuspecting police officers. They will search as much and as well as they can, but the forest will keep part of her hidden and safe.

Marie, in another life, had been a prostitute, not a very good one. She had lasted three months before picking the wrong guy, and then she lasted two scream-filled days. He would admit later, to himself, that with her he had been too sloppy, too eager. Perhaps if she had just been found earlier, then there would have been enough evidence on her to ... well it is too late for that now.

A forensic anthropologist will state that the skeleton is most likely to be female, aged between seventeen and twenty-five, he bases this on the fusion of epiphyses in the humerus. The anthropologist determines that the victim has been in the ground for anything between two and five years. Cause of death: undetermined, foul play suspected. She had been dumped naked, they are sure of that much. No fragments or shreds of clothing could be found close by, nothing that could be used to identify Jane Doe number 217. No purse, no jewellery, no shoes, no skin. Trauma to the bone was detailed, several chew marks caused by animals. Then several marks across the two of the metacarpal bones, bones that had previously formed the left hand, notches on the bones that had not been caused by a fang.

In desperation, they will hire a facial reconstruction expert, who, to her credit, will do a good job. The first time he saw the facial sketch, blaring across the screen in an appeal for information, he was shocked. He wasn't expecting her to be found, didn't expect any of his early ones to be found. The second time he saw the picture ... the second time he masturbated. He, like a million other viewers were accosted with the image of not-quite-Marie Eine, staring at them with vacant reconstructed eyes and a pronounced jaw. He and five other clients recognised her but none of them ever cared to admit it.

He is busy now, too busy to care that much about Marie Eine. At the moment he is busy jogging, he goes jogging most nights. Surveying new areas, measuring the pros and cons of the next possible dump site, planning and playing out every possible element in his head. There is another girl, a slender, dark-haired girl. She smiles at him, in that accidental moment when opposing joggers' eyes meet. He can smell the sweet scent of her hair as she passes. He can almost sense her desperation too, the silent prayer, *oh God, please let him notice me*. He can see that her looks, her pleasing but not beautiful looks, are starting to blemish. That her jogging routine was only taken up recently in a futile battle against her growing bulges. She isn't special enough for him to waste too much time on but she would be fun to play with for a little while. He has some bigger plans but they need a little more time, a little more preparation. He needs this now! It has been two long, agonising months since his last quick fix.

Maybe for this one he will suggest a picnic. A romantic little lunch in a secluded area, she might say yes to this, she gives off the impression she is married. The ring on the finger is a dead giveaway but that smile suggests she is willing to play. Particularly if he asks the right way, really playing up the bashful yet handsome side, trick the silly bitch into saying yes. She wouldn't say no anyway not to him, bitch is practically begging for it. They were all begging for it. There she is now,

21

right on time, quick check to make sure they are really alone and then slow down a little.

Smile that shy boy smile and say, "Hi there."

Stella hoists her short red skirt higher, revealing even more tantalising thigh. Worked all day, whored all night! The white powder is calling to her and well, fuck it she has earned it now, hasn't she? Last fucking bugger tipped her well, hurriedly shoving the cash towards her before retreating, ashamed, back to his fucking family. Maybe one more, she's got to eat tonight. She stubs her cigarette out on a *Missing* poster, mashing the hot residue straight into the photograph, burning away Adelina Sasha's features.

She poses against a wall, a wall coated with sperm and urine. A moment passes then her scuffed red leather boots twist as she slides back down the slime. Her short red skirt rising higher and higher, revealing more bruised and needle poked thighs. Deflated withered breasts being slowly coated with warm blood.

She is still warm when they find her. They snap shots with camera phones before walking on with a laugh. But someone eventually will call the police. The call goes out and the rats gather round. A dead prostitute surrounded by shrunken condoms, approximately twenty this time, more trash and probably a rat carcass or two. More bagging and processing to do, each bag to be sealed with biohazard tape. Each item marked, recorded and photographed before being removed. The entire scene has to be preserved, even the slime, the filth and the sperm. The officers work quietly and solemnly, despite the hazards, despite the care they take, despite the hundreds of photographs, despite the many pairs of eyes searching, combing through, despite everything they miss a small tarnished object trodden into the mud.

Fletcher and Bullface are on their way, despite their already full case load. Six months ago they were called to the scene of Fran Lizzie Taylor, a girl who grotesquely died with the number 22 carved in her hand. Now they have been called to the scene of Stella McQam, a contrived prostitute with a 28 hurriedly carved into her right hand.

"Victim's name is Stella McQam, got an ID off her prints. She has been busted twice for prostitution." Fletcher pauses, rubbing his eyes with frustration "There is a possibility we are looking at a copycat killer. Fran Lizzie's number was carved on her left hand and her throat was cut. Stella's number was carved into her right hand and she was stabbed, just a few inches above the heart."

"I didn't think the number on the previous vic had made the news." Bullface mutters.

"It didn't." Oh great, If this was a copycat, then someone else was betraying them.

"So where do you want to start?" Bullface asks with absolutely no hint of enthusiasm.

Fletcher doesn't feel like starting, he feels like going back home. Not that he would admit this to anyone but he just wants to crawl away, hide under his duvet. Fran Lizzie had not been a lone death and now there were other issues he dared not voice. He feels disturbed, disturbed by the crowd who have gathered close by, held back by officers and tape. He catches glimpses of their conversations, their disdain for a bint who probably deserved it. He feels disturbed by the noise of the traffic going past, as if this was just another normal day. His eyes are firmly stuck to the blood stain. His nose is even insisting it can still smell the coppery scent of blood, bile rises in his throat. He can hear Bullface giving orders, dispatching officers to seize camera phones, obtain warrants for any CCTV footage within a mile of the accident. The assailant was likely to be on foot, Stella's blood anointing his clothes. He can hear all this but all he can think is that he wants to go home.

Fletcher doesn't go home. He spends the day interviewing potential eyewitnesses who have seen nothing, but are still eager to talk. Eyewitnesses who in turn are trying to discover more details from him. They are trying to find out everything he knows.

"Was she, like, mutilated?"

"Yeah, I heard 'bout her. Bloke kicked the shit outta her, right?"

Questions like that are asked to encourage Fletcher to reply, correcting their guesses, in a superior I-know-more-than-you sort of way. Fletcher isn't that stupid but knows that replies like, "I am not prepared to discuss that with you," are magically turned into "Yes, that's what happened." Denials are always taken as encouragements. Questions like, "Have you noticed anyone behaving suspiciously lately?" are always met with a flurry of answers, *this is the bad part of the city, almost every customer is suspicious.* Some customers were suspicious just because they acted polite or because they didn't smoke. Fletcher now has several pages of notes and some reluctantly handed over video footage of the suspicious people, people he suspects are probably just eccentric rather than suspicious. Other interviewing teams will bring in similar characters; each one has to be checked thoroughly. Bullface has been shadowing him on these interviews and is equally depressed. They both sit, watching the video feed that caught Stella's last smoke before disappearing down the dark alleyway. Over and over on a loop, she goes in and dies. The assailant had entered and left via another alleyway, into the maze of a city, avoiding the cameras. Their shift is nearly over but overtime is beckoning.

"He could be anyone. Stella was known to take on any..." Fletcher pauses while deciding on the best way to phrase this, "...client. No one saw anyone wearing blood-stained clothes, he could have dumped them."

"I had a team collect all the bins within a mile radius. They are going through the contents at the moment. I am going over to supervise."

Fletcher is hit by a tidal wave of stench as he follows Bullface into the room. The fumes of sickly sweet cans of fizzy drinks are battling against the stench of decomposing foods with just a few hints of cigarettes. One of the older officers looks up and grimly welcomes them to hell. They had collected twelve overflowing bags and two officers are still on the scene, going through a rotting skip. Afterwards, those two officers will be met with sprays of air freshener wherever they go. Each bag's location and time of collection has been recorded and the unlucky officers pull evidence out of the Pandora's box of rubbish, while others record the contents. So far one bloody tissue has been recovered, four bloody needles and two suspiciously smelling packages. The officers' jokes are best left unsaid, particularly the one about Constable Tichan's mother.

Kain has just lit the fifth cigarette of the day. That's how time passes, cigarettes and orc deaths. Kain hasn't even moved for four hours, keeping eyes firmly fixed on the door. Waiting and watching, not knowing what's happening outside in the real world and not caring.

The teenager just feels like walking, he has been walking for days now. Sure he feels a little thirsty, but there is bound to be water somewhere. Sure he feels a little hungry but it just doesn't matter. He is outside! Outside where he belongs, out in the fields, in the woods and he can walk forever! Elation fills his every vein as he runs, hollering through an empty field. Laughing and shouting at the sky. It is only out here that he feels free; he thinks he should just quit, quit living with his mother, quit begging for work and just live out here. The Earth will take care of him. It will be all right, it will be. His eyes stray across the field, attracted to the dark mass that lies there. The Earth has decided to give him the girl of his dreams. He lets out a big cry of happiness and begins to run toward her. Here is another person, a girl, someone else who also likes being outside. Someone who feels the same way!

From a distance she looks pretty, just lying in the sun. He runs closer, intrigued, until he realises she isn't moving. He can hear a peculiar sound, a sound which comes from thousands of maggots feasting as one, a mushy pit of rice munching swiftly at her face, arms and stomach. He stares frozen at the carnage. He wants to kick off every last one of those maggots but dares not touch, dares not move. Her mouth is frozen open in a death scream, choked back by squirming white grubs.

He had found his dream girl three days after she had died. He will be with the police soon, still shaking. His mouth permanently fixed in a choke. He will cry all through the interviews, cry as they take his prints. Then it will really hit, and he will start screaming. Crying and screaming for days as he is signed in "for observation". He will still be crying four months later.

Just hours after the body was abandoned, the insects began to multiply, encouraged by the beautiful warm day. Attracted by the aroma of blood they lay eggs into unprotesting festering wounds. These eggs took a day to hatch, releasing squiggles of white flesh which started their migration through the decomposing body. As maggots cannot chew through skin and because the victim is found with a small colony feasting on her left hand, it suggests that she has another number. However, the cuts could have been inflicted by animals, they could be defensive wounds torn open by feasting flies. She had cuts across her stomach and arms, also filled with frenzied banqueting bugs, none of the other victims so far had shown such mutilations. She cannot be linked to the murders of Fran Lizzie Taylor or Stella McQam just yet. The victim's small purse was found, carefully tucked into place underneath a red lacy bra. The purse is empty, except for one Polaroid. The victim's money is currently being exchanged for a round at the local pub, as he treats several off-duty policemen to a pint of their choice. Her credit cards and driving licence are carefully locked in his safe.

The Polaroid is of a young woman, lying naked on the ground. The woman is covered in bruises and deep interlacing cuts, twisted jagged lines slashed across her throat. Her hands have been carefully placed across her chest, the palms face down so that the number two so cautiously carved, can be clearly seen. The young woman clearly isn't the same victim. The image is why Fletcher and Bullface have been called.

"Right, what do we know?"

Oh, hello, Victoria, nice to see you too, Fletcher thinks before responding, "No ID, the victim is still a Jane Doe. Michaels is going through the missing persons lists. The victim was most likely killed here."

Fletcher eyes up the landscape, it looks too beautiful. The fields are beaming serenely as the August sun begins to set, casting a brilliant orange glare over the postcard image. Fletcher stands alert, his hairs on end as his ears tell him that this scene is too quiet, too eerie, it is as if the nearby forest is eavesdropping on their conversation.

"Something the matter?" Bullface asks, with little actual concern in her voice.

"Just wondering what she was doing out here. This is a very secluded area." Bullface shrugs, as if to say if we knew why she was out here, we wouldn't be out here.

"Do you think she is connected to Fran Taylor and Stella McQam?" Fletcher asks quietly.

"Right now we don't even know if Fran and Stella are connected. There is a possibility though as the victim sustained trauma to her left hand, insect damage has made it impossible to tell if she also had a number carved into her hand. But then that picture..." her voice trails off before quietly stating, "...there is a possibility they are connected, the victim in the photo had a number 2, Fran a 22, and Stella a 28. If the photograph was left by the same killer, then he is not just carving their ages. But without knowing what number had been carved into this victim's hand..." another pause, there are some things Bullface just doesn't feel like spelling out to Fletcher. She wants to know he is capable of doing his job "You do know what this could mean, don't you?"

"What?" Maybe Fletcher does know, but he doesn't want to say, saying it out loud could make it true.

"There could be another twenty-four victims already."

"Shit."

There seems little to do now, the night shift is slowly taking over, Michaels is still ploughing through *Missings*, and the victim would not be autopsied until the morning. Both officers are tired, tomorrow morning is already beckoning with more work. Fletcher heads home, but Bullface, well Bullface doesn't head home, there seems little point. At home there will be a husband more interested in the television than her and two sons who are usually absent. On the rare occasions they are home, the house is rocked with blaring music and arguments. She can stand them on most nights but tonight, for a while, she needs silence. She needs to think.

Instead Bullface goes to her second home. She and her husband buy several old houses a year, slowly reviving them for rent or resale. Her husband retired a few years ago and it seems to keep him occupied. He plasters, she paints.

Usually Bullface likes painting, an activity that allows her to be perfect and precise, allows her mind to wander, time to run through her active cases, looking for mistakes or missed leads and time to reanalyse actions. Tonight is different. She can feel the eyes watching her again, eyes of so many female ghosts hiding just out of sight. Every brush stroke echoes the same question in her head. What is the point? Splat! What is the point? What is the point? Until she gives up, wearily sitting down on the dust sheets, head lying in paint splattered hands, just trying to find the strength to go home.

The night brings forth whispers, stronger allegations against The Krill. Fran Lizzie has been brought back to life by gossip. The police phone lines are again jammed with anxious relatives and journalists eager for more insight. The focus is on the mutilated victim apparently found in a church graveyard/skip/forest/lake rather than on the prostitute Stella McQam. Fear has returned, wives refuse to walk to work alone in the morning, mothers argue with daughters, the restrictions for protection are always misunderstood and always end in door slams.

The morning does bring one good thing: an identity for the

newest Jane Doe. Michaels has spent most of her night going through page after page of smiling vacant faces on her screen contrasting them against a close up of Jane's decomposing features. Michaels was rarely bothered by these images. She'd been injured two years ago and was now desk bound, so most of the missing came to her. It was something for her to do, just a job. At first, the *Missings'* smiling faces had bothered her but now she is used to it. The decomposing face, however, that is something she wants to get off her desk as soon as possible. But now Michaels is owed gratitude because thanks to her, the numberless nameless victim can be identified as Adelina Sasha.

Adelina's husband, Jack Sasha, will confirm her identity. Jack, Adelina's widower but he will always call himself her husband. Later on, much later on, ten years later he will still say he is married. He will rarely add "But she is dead now," not wanting to see the gleam of sadness, pity or even hope in the questioner's eyes. Not wanting to encourage the "How did she die?" Or an "I am sorry." Or even an "Are you seeing anyone now?" usually asked playfully, the asker thrusting shrivelled breasts forward, as if to encourage the asking of a phone number.

The morgue assistants try to be tactful. They have been careful not to show him anything other than her face, but the sight of her lying there her eyes permanently closed, is enough to spark a flame. Jack has spent his life as an angry man, his passionate anger was what made Adelina fall for him in the first place. Maybe she considered cheating on him just to reignite that dying flame, but she, unlike the morgue assistants, would have known to move away very quickly when that vein throbs on his temple, when the left eyebrow twitches. Jack is quickly led into an interview room, to become someone else's problem before he breaks anything else.

Fletcher offers him a drink, offers to call someone for Jack, but such offerings are barely acknowledged. Jack sits, forcefully holding himself down to the chair, shaking slightly. Fletcher tries to give Jack silence and time, enough time to realise what is going on. Fletcher is also a little impatient, time cannot be wasted. Finally, he breaks the sullen silence, announces the time and date of the interview into the awaiting video camera and begins.

"I am Detective Sergeant Aaron Fletcher and this is my partner Detective Sergeant Victoria Bull... rush." Fletcher quickly continues before Bullface notices the pause. "We will be investigating your wife's case. We need to ask you a few questions." Fletcher pauses uncertainly, Jack still barely acknowledges his existence. His anger slowly deflating second by second, leaving behind an empty hollow man.

"How long were you and Adelina married?"

"Thirteen years." A defeated mumble.

"Were you having any problems in your marriage?"

Jack's eyebrow twitches again. "No."

Fletcher thinks this may be a sensitive subject for him, rarely did someone answer so abruptly. Jack's posture hints that he might be waiting for the right moment to strike.

"OK, let's talk a little bit about the day she disappeared." Fletcher hopes to calm Jack down before coming back to his previous marital issues. There is nothing on record to say that they had an unhappy marriage, no charges of assault, no divorce pending, but still, there are always some secrets hidden away. He chooses to use words such as 'disappeared' rather than 'left' as it implied she had wanted to leave. Little points to try and reassure Jack Sasha that, at the moment, Fletcher is on his side.

"The morning she disappeared, do you remember what had happened?"

Silence.

"Mr Sasha?"

Silence.

"Was she getting ready to go to work?"

"My wife takes Fridays off, so she didn't have to go to work. She still got up with me and we had breakfast together."

"What did she have to eat?"

"Grapefruit." Evidently Jack Sasha is a man of few grunts.

"What was she wearing?"

"She was still in her nightgown."

"What time was this?"

"'Bout eight, eight fifteen."

"Had she told you what she planned to do that day?"

"She was going to clean and then meet a friend for lunch – like I said in the Missings' Report."

"Had she said who she was meeting?"

"No."

"Did she usually go out for lunch on her own?"

"Yes."

"Had she seemed emotional that morning?"

"She was an emotional person." Jack Sasha does not want to relinquish the last private memories of her, doesn't want another man to see the emotions she always showed him in the morning. Jack half sighs, half chokes an unwanted tear before continuing. "She was happy. She liked the mornings."

"So she was in a good mood? She didn't seem tearful or upset?"

"No!" A whisper of anger is laced in that line, Jack Sasha's eyes meet with Fletcher's in a flash of venom, not liking what Fletcher could be implying.

"Where did your wife like to spend her time?"

"She is at work five days a week, she works Sunday to Thursday. She usually comes straight home, most nights she will go out for a jog, Fridays she meets up with her friends, Saturdays she spends with me." He talks mechanically, Jack is giving Fletcher the I-don't-like-you-but-I-will-answer-your-questions look.

"Did she have any reason to be out in the countryside?"

"No."

"Not even to go jogging?"

"I don't know her jogging route."

"Are any of her items missing? Like her toothbrush or any of her favourite clothes?"

"She wasn't going to leave me," Jack snaps.

"Please answer the question."

"No, the only thing missing is her car." The police have already been alerted about Adelina Sasha's missing car. Michaels is contacting the relevant tow away companies.

"When did you realise she was missing?"

"She wasn't there when I got home at six. She is always home before me."

"Even on her days off?"

"Yes."

"What did you do?"

"I phoned some of her friends and family, made sure she wasn't running late. Tried her mobile too but that went straight to voice mail."

"Did anyone say where she was?"

"No."

"When did you contact the police?"

"The next morning, when she still hadn't come home." Jack's voice is shaky now, it is beginning to hit him that his wife would never be coming home.

"Who was your wife particularly close to? We would also like to interview them, if possible."

Jack hesitates, his grief-infused mind can only recall

Adelina's face not her friends. It takes a few silent minutes while his face visibly works for a name.

"Who is she close to in her family?" Fletcher decides to help him a little.

"Her mother, Adelina is an only child. She and her mother are pretty close."

"Is she close to anyone at work?"

"I don't ... I don't think she is."

"Any of her friends?"

"Anna."

"What's Anna's last name?"

"Stevenson."

After a few moments of silence, Fletcher asks, "Did your wife know Fran Lizzie Taylor?"

"I ... I don't know, my wife has many friends."

There is a swish as Bullface pulls out a photo of the living Fran Lizzie.

Jack barely glances at it before replying, "I don't recognise her."

"What were you doing on March 9th?"

"I don't remember, how is this important?"

"It was a Friday night. Please try to think."

"If it was a Friday night I probably was with Adelina. What does this have to do with anything?"

"Did your wife know Stella McQam?"

"She has a friend called Stella, I don't remember her last name, I don't think it's McQam though." There is a pause, Jack is trying to figure out what this idiot might be implying. "Why? What do these women have to do with this?"

"We think they might be connected."

"Are they suspects? Do you think these women killed..." Jack chokes on his wife's name.

Fletcher takes advantage of the pause to interrupt. "No, we don't think they are suspects. Do you recognise this woman?"

Bullface pulls out another cropped photo, the picture that had been found in Adelina Sasha's purse. They have cropped the image carefully so only the victim's face can be seen.

"No, what do these women have to do with my wife?" Anger re-laces his voice. He looks up at the two grim faces.

"Mr Sasha." Fletcher begins quietly.

"Do you believe him?" Fletcher asks Bullface tentatively.

"For now," she mutters. They are watching Jack Sasha leaving the station, his escorts closely shielding him from the waiting press. Jack still looks angry, like he might go for anyone who gets too close. He just needs an excuse to take a swing. Through the open window, the calls of the press drift in.

"Mr Sasha! Is it true they found your wife?"

"Was she mutilated?"

"Mr Sasha! Mr Sasha!"

"Do you have anything to say to your wife's murderer?"

Jack Sasha stops despite the urging of his escorts, slowly turns to face the luckless reporter. Bullface holds her breath, readying to run to the escorts' aid.

Sasha faces the camera. "I will find you," he hisses. Every word is uttered clearly. "Everything you did to her, I will do to you." He leans closer into the camera, the footage picking up every throbbing vein around his bloodshot eyes. Flecks of spit hit the lens as he thunders, "I will find you." He is hurried into an awaiting car by two very anxious escorts. The footage will make the six o'clock news, along with the film of Adelina's mother weeping hysterically for twenty seconds.

Jack Sasha had, before he exited so dramatically, graciously provided the officers with Anna Stevenson's contact details. She sits now in Jack's place in the conference room. Her mascara has run in thick black lines down her face, smearing into foundation with every tissue wipe. Little drips of make-up cascade onto her bright-yellow shirt as Anna's face falls apart with every tear.

"I just can't believe anyone would hurt Adelina. She's such a great..."

Fletcher clears his throat slightly nervously. Bullface fidgets in a slight discomfort.

"Ms Stevenson, I would like to ask you a few questions about your relationship with Adelina Sasha, if I may?"

"Of course, anything to help Adelina."

Bullface rolls her eyes inwardly at the cliché, she does try to be sympathetic but thinks maybe Anna Stevenson is a little too much. Particularly since Anna seemed almost flirtatious in her grief. Flirtatious with Fletcher by the way, not with Bullface.

"How did you meet Adelina Sasha?"

"I met her when we were in university, we both took business studies together." The tears are slowly drying up. Anna rubs her face with a tissue as if suddenly self-conscious. Bullface really wants to tell her that Fletcher is married.

"So how long have you known her?"

"Nearly erm ... nearly twenty years now."

"So a long time then, you must have known her pretty well." Fletcher tries to make himself as friendly as possible, much to Bullface's disdain.

"Yes we are..." pause, then the invariable second cliché, "... we were very close."

Family and friends, Bullface thinks, sometimes just seemed to be following a script. That old dramatisation where suddenly they start correcting their speech, going back to correct present tense to become past, the endless 'she is' then a pause, 'she was'. Was it the sudden realisation of the lost? Or maybe the juxtaposition of suddenly losing someone, someone special crossed with the chance of being famous, of being involved in something considered to be dramatic. Maybe this juxtaposition commanded that they all follow the same script. Then maybe, Bullface relents, they just don't know what they are saying, the correcting is just automatic. Jack Sasha hadn't used such rewording, suggesting that to him, in his mind, his wife is still very much alive. Bullface, after seeing Jack's behaviour does not want to be around when the realisation of Adelina's death finally hits him.

"So you knew her before she met Jack Sasha?"

"Yes, I was the one who introduced them." There is a slight bitterness in her voice.

"Would you say they had a happy marriage?"

"Well, Jack can sometimes be a little, well, extreme, but I think overall she had a happy marriage." There is a touch of bitterness there again. Bullface wonders if the unmarried Anna was maybe slightly jealous, but then Bullface always thinks the worst of people.

"Did she mention any problems to you?"

There is a hesitation, a pause, then Anna slowly shakes her permed hair. "She was generally happy."

"So she wasn't having any kind of problems? No financial problems? No problems at work?"

Anna's slightly uneasy look is betraying her. "Erm ... not really," comes the weak reply.

Fletcher's eyes meet hers with a gentle glare.

"She was just feeling a bit ... well old. It was her birthday last month and, well, she kept saying she was the wrong side of thirty now. She will be forty in two years and she was thinking of changing her career. You know, the average, 'I don't know where I am going' sort of thing. But she was still happy, she loved Jack."

"So she has been a little emotional lately?"

"Since she took up jogging she started to improve. I think the exercise was really doing her some good. She used to talk about..." A sudden stop as Anna realises that she is about to betray her friend.

"What did she used to talk about?" It hasn't quite clicked with Fletcher.

"There was a guy she would see while out jogging, a youngish guy. I think she might have been a little flattered by his attention. It was all harmless though, Adelina would never cheat on Jack." She didn't add that Adelina may have been afraid of what Jack might do if he found out.

"Was this the person she was meant to be meeting on Friday?"

"Oh no, like I said, Adelina was flattered but she would never cheat on Jack."

"Did she mention who she was meeting?"

"She was meant to be meeting me at three, we were going to do a little shopping."

"What did you do when she didn't turn up?"

"I rang her a few times, but she didn't answer. I just thought she had forgotten. We didn't have definite plans anyway. It wasn't till Jack called that I realised she was actually missing."

"You didn't tell Mr Sasha that it was you Adelina was meant to be meeting?"

"I thought I did, but I don't know, he was really panicked. I guess he was scared she had left him or something. He might not have heard me or something."

"Do you know the name of the guy Adelina would meet while jogging?"

"No, I don't think she knew his name, it was just a little fun that's all. She wouldn't have hurt Jack or anything. Adelina used to be very pretty, I think she was just flattered that someone was noticing her again."

"Do you know what this guy looked like?"

"No, I never met him." Realisation hits her, her smudged eyes open wide, the pudgy mouth forming a little O. "You think he might have…"

"We need to look into every possibility," Fletcher says gently.

In Anna's mind, however, the mystery is solved, it was a jogger who killed Adelina. Jack is cleared of all suspicions, it was a mysterious stranger who killed Adelina. A story that would be over-romanticised as Anna met her other friends for drinks and shared gossip and tears for Adelina, also strategic plans on how to 'comfort' Jack Sasha.

What Fletcher asks next only added extra juice to the gossip. "Did Adelina have any contact with Fran Lizzie Taylor?"

"That name does sound familiar … I don't think Adelina knew anyone called Fran…" Anna doesn't want to admit that she doesn't know all of Adelina's friends. Then it clicks, her eyes open wide again. "She was the girl who was murdered, about six months ago. Wasn't she?"

"So Adelina had no connection with Fran?"

"Do you think it was the same guy? Adelina was so scared when that happened, she didn't want to go out for weeks afterwards."

"Please answer my question, Ms Stevenson."

"No, I don't think she ever met Fran, if she did, she didn't mention it to me." The tone is slightly indignant as if to imply there may be other things Adelina hadn't mentioned to her.

Bullface again produces the altered photograph. "Do you recognise this girl?"

Anna gives it a long hard look, her fingers shaking on the table with fear and excitement. She is actually seeing photos! She thought that only happened in crime shows, she could be famous. Then there is a growing fear, rumours of what happened to Adelina had reached Anna, the rumours that the sight of her had made a grown man cry, and the police thought there could be other victims. That meant a...

"She looks a little familiar, I don't know why. Has she been on telly or something? I don't think Adelina knew her though, unless she worked with her."

"Try to think," Fletcher advises patiently. Bullface stirs slightly, if Anna recognised the unknown girl in the photograph ... well it might open up a new lead or two, new possibilities. These women had to have something in common, it was just a case of finding it.

"No, I really don't know. Sorry."

Fletcher presses a business card into Anna's eager hand, with the statutory, "If you remember, please give me a call."

CHAPTER FOUR

"OK, let's go over what we know so far." Fletcher and Bullface sit in the briefing room, six coffees and piles of paperwork spread across the table. Two other blank-faced detectives sit opposite.

"First known victim was Fran Lizzie Taylor, aged twenty-two. She was found with the number 22 carved into her left hand. The mutilation was inflicted by a scalpel or a small knife, post mortem. She was found on March 9th, at 8am, having been killed maybe six or seven hours before. She was fully clothed with no signs of sexual assault, no defensive wounds. Her throat had been slit, death was near instantaneous. She was found in an isolated area, thrown over a five-foot fence." Fletcher states all this mechanically.

Bullface continues in a similar monotone. "The dumpsite felt planned; although her purse is still missing. We think this was an intentional murder rather than a robbery gone wrong, I think he took the purse for a token. Because everything seemed planned, we are presuming he is of rational mind, the killings are not the work of someone in a frenzy. This implies that he is an organised killer, who knows what he is doing. The victim had been thrown over a five foot fence; this would take someone of a strong build and height."

Bullface pauses to sip her coffee, wishing it were something stronger and warmer.

Fletcher takes up the report. "Several fibres had been found on the victim's body, three of them were a match to the pub seating, two are black seventy-five per cent cotton, twenty-five per cent polyester fibres, and one is unknown. No DNA has been found on the victim, evidence found at the scene is circumstantial. As you can see," Fletcher pauses to show them one of the many photographs of Fran Lizzie's demise, "several cigarettes were found on the scene. DNA has been recovered but nothing is a match to anyone in our system. Other items found on the scene are listed here. All these items have been fingerprinted and DNA has been taken from them, again no matches in the system. As you can see a purse was found by our officers, in this river." He points again to the photograph. "Along with a briefcase, neither of these items belongs to Fran Lizzie Taylor, both were reported as stolen weeks before the attack."

"Do you have any suspects on this case?" one of the detectives asks, the other frantically scribbling notes.

"Our first suspect was Fran's boyfriend, Steven, but he has been cleared by his alibi, he was working that night, around twenty miles away. There is no chance he could have slipped out and killed her. Fran's flatmate was also investigated, but she doesn't seem likely."

One eyebrow is questioningly raised at this.

"Fran's flatmate is five foot four, she would not have been able to lift and throw Fran over a five foot fence. Her flatmate has no alibi though."

"Anyone else?"

"Fran had been out drinking with one of her work colleagues, she left the pub alone and no one had been seen following her. At the moment we have no other suspects. None of the DNA found on the scene is a match to Fran's family, boyfriend, flatmate or work colleagues.

"The second victim to be found was Stella McQam, aged thirty-seven. Found yesterday. She had a number 28 carved into her right hand. Victim was a prostitute, found in a busy location, dumped in an alleyway, fully clothed, obvious signs of sexual penetration. She has been processed and the DNA is now being sent off, though it could be several months before we see the result. She had been stabbed twice in succession. Her number was inflicted shortly before or during death." Bullface pauses again, collecting her thoughts, allowing Fletcher to take over.

"Because the attack happened in a busy area, we believe that the assailant may have dumped some of his clothes. We had officers collect the bins within a mile radius, they are currently going through them as we speak. We have seized CCTV footage and recorded eyewitness statements but so far no one has seen anyone suspicious.

"The next victim has been identified as Adelina Sasha. She was killed three or four days before Stella. Adelina was partly decomposed when she was found, she has some trauma to her left hand. As you can see, insect damage means that we cannot assume or deny that she may have been numbered. Adelina was thirty-eight, she had been reported missing by her husband. Victim was found partly dressed. She was still wearing a black skirt, white shirt, underwear and shoes. Her shirt had been undone and there were several slashes to her stomach as well as to her arms and face. Her autopsy shows that she had been drinking shortly before death, stomach contents included several sandwiches and some fruit. She was killed shortly after eating. Cause of death was a slit throat, like Fran Lizzie Taylor.

"She was found in a secluded area, out in the fields. Her car is still missing, I have put out an APB to keep an eye out for it."

The scribbler pauses. "Any chance she was killed by her husband?"

"Slim chance, her husband was at work at the estimated time of death. He can clearly be seen on his company's CCTV footage for most of the day. The victim's body indicates she had been killed where she was found. Officers are checking into his financial accounts. We are also appealing for eyewitnesses to come forward.

"We interviewed one of Adelina's friends, there is a possibility that Adelina may have been having an affair with someone she met while jogging. The friend could not give us any more details.

"What connects Adelina to this case is a Polaroid found in her purse. Adelina's purse was empty by the way, it seems the assailant had taken the contents. Jack Sasha identified the purse as belonging to Adelina. No fingerprints have been found on the purse or the photograph."

A copy of the Polaroid is again pulled out and passed across to the officers. One takes it with a grimace.

"There is little possibility that the girl is alive. The assailant obviously wants us to know that there are other victims out there. She may have been his second victim."

"Any idea what the numbers mean?"

"The most obvious one is that he is numbering each kill. This is hard to determine because we don't know what Adelina Sasha's number was or if she had a number. If the assailant is using a code then it is not an alphabetical code as Stella McQam was number 28 and as we know the alphabet contains only twenty-six letters." Bullface feels the need to state the obvious, as she considers most of her co-workers to be idiots. "Since the numbers inflicted on the victims changes from left to right hands, there could be a possibility of two assailants. One carving on the left hand, one carving on the right, however, no other

44

evidence can support or confirm this so far. But the difference in dump sites and modes of kill also suggests this."

"The girl in this picture, has she been identified?"

"Not as yet, we are planning to include her in the media campaign."

"She looks a little familiar." A long uncomfortable pause hovers as the luckless officer tries to recall.

The other officer interrupts with an authoritative, "If there is a possibility there are twenty-four other bodies out there, then we need to look for them."

The city is screaming with rumours. The death of Stella McQam had not caused that much concern to begin with, but then someone realised that her death was linked to the two other deaths, possibly even three or nine, or even twenty! other deaths. The whispers rapidly begin to swell combining with murmurs about mutilations, the bafflement of the police and the possibility of even more victims. Some say that an underground bomb shelter had been found out in the fields, filled with sacrificed children. Other rumours take the Blackbeard approach that all the women had been married, in secret, to a mysterious man who literally stole their hearts. The women had been found missing their eyes/teeth/hearts/fingers/toes. More postulated on the murderer himself, that Jack Sasha had broken down and confessed that Steve was his secret boyfriend. Fran Lizzie had caught them together and her death had been an accident. It had been a local politician, covering up his string of affairs. The bookie's favourite, The Krill, was still the prime suspect, casting a metaphysical dark shadow over every conversation. What should have been a tragic death for Adelina Sasha turned into a romanticised, over-exaggerated death. What should have been a period of mourning for Jack Sasha turned into a hunting party, where over-eager blamers, reporters and not so altruistic comforters tracked him down and shrieked him into isolation.

Kain knows nothing of this, has not yet heard of the deaths and is still smoking quietly in the darkness, completely unaware of the watching eyes.

Elizabeth Mitchell is also watching someone. She is standing next to her window, her wrinkled thin claws holding back a purple velvet drape, allowing her a full view of the house opposite. A clipboard rests on the coffee table next to her, carefully but shakily divided into columns of comings and goings. As a tall, dark-clothed young man exits the house with a customary slam, she carefully notes the time and then sits back. She closes her eyes and listens to the whispering wireless as she carefully contemplates her next move.

Bullface and Fletcher split up after the meeting. Adelina Sasha's car has finally been found, Fletcher is to examine any findings. Bullface does not want to sit and wait for the investigator's report. She is going to check on the rubbish collected from the Stella McQam case. She is a little unnerved, not that Bullface admits to these things, but there is a small alarm bell ringing. It is the girl in the photograph. The photograph they had found with Adelina Sasha, the girl with a number 2 cut into her hands. She is familiar to so many people, but they still don't have as much as a name. She does seem a little familiar to Bullface too, but why? Michaels had unhappily trailed through two years' worth of *Missings* but no match. The victim's eyes are closed so there are one or two that might have been her, but unlikely. With no body, there is no way of being sure. Bullface feels that the assailant is testing them, taunting them with someone who may not even be real. Bullface has seen a lot of photo manipulation over the years but this one ... she is not quite sure. She thinks it is real but then there is still the nagging feeling. She is definitely missing something.

Six long smelly hours are spent going through the garbage. A hundred more days are required for the DNA testing phase. The burnt Missing poster with Adelina Sasha's scorched face has been noted, the offending cigarette has been processed for DNA. They are still hoping that maybe there will be a match, something from Fran Lizzie's scene matching to Stella McQam's. Just one lucky break. It would be a long wait to find out. The Missing poster bothers Bullface, is it a message from the killer? Was he mocking them with half-burnt clues? It feels like he is mocking them with every kill, always whispering in the darkness, hinting at what they can't see. Bullface feels stupid for not being able to see the links, and she hates being made to feel stupid. Tension and anger are buried deep in her forehead, a permanent scowl has set heavily in her eyebrows.

There are several pieces of bloody materials, one bloody tissue and four bloody needles, but no clothes. The officers who had gone skip diving have come away with empty but contaminated hands. The two suspicious-smelling packages are also disappointing; one is a discarded rotting lunch and the other regurgitated materials from an unfortunate drunk.

Fletcher watches as the contents of Adelina's car are emptied and slowly processed. There are the usual tissues and CDs in the side door, spare coins in the cup holder, maps and messages in the glove box. Adelina kept her car clean and neat, the interior of the car had been vacuumed recently so the CSI were a little less hopeful about picking up some of the assailant's skin flakes or hairs, had he been in the car. At the moment the evidence is suggesting that Adelina had been alone in there.

What is interesting to Fletcher is the make-up bag tucked carefully under the passenger seat. The bag was filled with make-up supplies and little bottles of perfume, to him it confirms the idea that she may have been meeting a male friend rather than another female. He is now briefly eyeing Adelina's CDs. She was heavily into jazz whereas Fran Lizzie was definitely a pop girl. Fletcher doubted Stella would be that into music (he didn't know of her secret love for heavy metal). There just seemed to be nothing connecting these girls so far, except for their gender.

The car had been found, abandoned at a lay-by some twenty minutes away from her dump site. This part of the city isn't really the city as such. Surrounding fields and a large wood separate them from a nearby village. The fields are waiting, begging to be developed and built upon. In a few years' time that little village will be absorbed into the city as the population continues to rise. Bullface cynically sees the village as another den of thieves waiting to be enrolled. The fields and lack of land development means that there were few speed cameras out here, nothing to document Adelina's arrival or her attacker's departure. Another dead end.

A police officer pulls out a piece of paper, lost under the driver's seat. Scrawled across it in hurried handwriting read the number 282202...

Brandi Parr has heard the whispered rumours, everyone in her office has murmured something different, scaring each other at the coffee pot. Right now she can hear Marcella, on the desk opposite hers, pleading to an unknown.

"I don't care what time the game starts, please just pick me up, OK?"

Brandi doesn't have anyone to plead to, her last boyfriend is a year-old memory and her father is over a hundred miles away, bound to her nagging mother. Brandi doesn't care though, the likelihood of someone actually picking on her is low.

Brandi methodically chews on her lunch of lettuce leaves, despising the bland taste. She longs for a nice burger or even a Chinese takeaway. Oh how her mother would love that, she would be able to choose between the *"You are not taking care of yourself properly."* Or the *"How will you ever get a man if you a) don't learn to cook properly, b) keep piling on those pounds."* Inevitably ending with the *"You are not getting any younger, you know."*

Brandi viciously stabs another lettuce leaf.

Marcella's voice rises to a whining squeak. "Because I don't want to walk home alone, you heard what happened to those girls!" Marcella is close to tears.

Brandi feels a small stab of glee as Little Miss Perfect Marcella is brought down a peg or two.

"Fine! But if anything happens to me, you will be sorry!" With the tearful threat comes the dramatic disconnect and the slam as the mobile phone hits the table in anger.

Brandi quickly ducks her head, pretending to be engaged in her lettuce. The chubby girl next to Marcella slides over with tissues, advice and the sympathetic, "I will walk home with you." Which of course Marcella graciously accepts. Brandi chews another lettuce leaf thoughtfully. That is another thing, no one cares if she walks home alone but if Miss High and Mighty Marcella must, well, bring in the whole office as convoy! Can't let Marcella go home alone. The lettuce leaves are not the only thing leaving a bad taste in Brandi's mouth.

Fletcher stares at the bagged piece of paper, the one they had found in Adelina's car. 282202. Stella, 28; Fran, 22; Unknown girl, 02. 282202. His hands shake in excitement. Is this a piece of evidence that could connect the four girls? He does a quick second guess in his mind, 2-B, 8-H, 0-? All equals BHBB-B ... no that definitely doesn't mean anything. It could be in the right order – newest victim first ... was he just cataloguing his previous kills? But then 28 had been killed after Adelina. Did he know that they wouldn't find her car until after they found 28? How could he have known that?

Bullface leans over his shoulder, interrupting his thoughts. "Is it a phone number?" she asks in a bored tone.

"What?"

"Have you tried ringing that number?"

"Err..." Fletcher does not want to admit that he hadn't thought of that. Though it did lead to another possibility, that the assailant had given Adelina his phone number. Bullface pushes the phone towards him with contempt.

Bullface does want this to mean something, to be a clue of some sort but then the simplest explanation is usually the correct one, it always has to be considered. The writing to her suggested female more than male. Despite the obvious hurry the writer had been in, there was still a clear concise element to the numbers.

Fletcher dials, just willing Bullface to be wrong, just to show her he wasn't that incompetent. The phone rings and rings. Fletcher's heart gives a small lurch when a breathless female answers.

"Hello?"

"H-hello," Fletcher mutters, the answering female sounds slightly familiar.

The voice is almost flirtatious. "Who is this?"

"This is Detective Sergeant Aaron Fletcher, who am I speaking to?"

"Well hello, Mr Fletcher," says the voice eagerly. "This is Anna Stevenson. We met earlier."

In Fletcher's mind, there are a few possibilities. One, Anna Stevenson is the next targeted victim, the assailant may have left her number in the car on purpose. This theory is ruled out when Anna confirms she had changed her phone number recently and had written it down for Adelina.

Anna agrees to come back in so they can check the handwriting. "I can be there in ten minutes," she twinkles excitedly.

Possibility two, the assailant may have seen the number in Adelina's car and may still target Anna. Fletcher knows this is a weak possibility since the evidence is showing that the assailant had not in all likelihood, even entered the car. Still the paper will be fingerprinted just to make sure. The clearest prospect is that this was just coincidence. Fletcher does not like coincidences.

Bullface is no longer paying any attention to the phone call. Something has caught her eye. The alarm bells are shrieking. To Fletcher's surprise, she slowly stands up, and walks across the crowded sea of desks. The answer has been staring at them all for months now. Anna's question of *"Has she been on telly or something?"* makes sense now, because she had been on TV. She would look familiar to all the officers here because her face, her reconstructed face has been staring out at them all, watching them from a poster for weeks now. The victim in the photograph looks very similar to the Jane Doe 217. The one that had been found in the forest. The reconstructed facial image of the one who has not yet been identified, Victim number 2.

Fletcher wearily slides into his car. It is 7pm, his shift was meant to finish at five but ... well, everything just kept hitting. The Jane Doe

2 I 7 case has been passed over to them, not that there was much to pass over. The biggest, hardest hit is the fact that Jane Doe 2 I 7's estimated death was anything from three to five years. If she is victim number 2 and she was killed five years ago, then that strengthens the most stressing theory, that the assailant is actually numbering his kills not coding them. Stella McQam is victim number 28, meaning that in the period of three to five years, this man has killed twenty-eight people and they had only found four bodies. Fletcher's head is pounding, as he dry-swallows two aspirins from the emergency stash in his car. If Fran Lizzie is victim number 22 and she was killed just six months ago, then the assailant has killed six females in six months without being caught. How? The city is hiding the bodies somewhere but where? Bullface has put forward a theory of a mass grave site, somewhere remote and hidden and Fletcher feels now inclined to agree. The faceless females seem to be screaming at him, every time he tries to close his eyes and think.

Fletcher slowly drives home, every vein in his body is growling. Fletcher wants nothing more than to go to the nearest pub, order the strongest mind rotter and just keep drinking until all this goes away. He knows at home Claire will be waiting, ready to yell at him for coming home so late. Stabbing more thorns in his head with the crying and fresh new arguments. Maybe she won't be there, she may have vanished, to complain to her mother or friends about how her useless husband is never home, never did this or never fixed that. There would be flowers to buy, chocolates to console but still the silent treatment will last until this hell is over. Then again maybe Claire will be more supportive this time. Fear can do strange things to people and Claire might be too scared to go anywhere alone. Fletcher feels the panic began to rise, the bile leaning on the back of his throat. Claire did go places alone, she always said that she wasn't scared of anything. It is one of the things Fletcher likes about her, that she will take on anything. From sky diving to roller-blading, anything she is dared to do, she will do it. There is no stopping Claire, no scaring Claire ... which means that while everyone else starts to take precautions, watch their shadows, Claire will charge straight out into the open, declaring that she is not afraid. That she can take on any man. Fletcher has seen what happens to those who have taken on this man and ... and ... how can he tell Claire to be careful? She will just look at him with scorn in her eyes and tell him life is too short to be afraid. If Fletcher is to keep on working overtime then Claire will be on her own more and more. Maybe the assailant is watching her right now. Fletcher's foot automatically presses harder on the accelerator. His head pulls into a tight vice of worry. Could be watching her right now. She could already be dead! A car suddenly pulls out in front of him, causing him to slam down hard on the brake. The cursing drivers behind him protest with horn blasts. His heart is palpitating erratically, his hands shake as he restarts the engine and takes a deep breath.

His wife is waiting at the door, with an angry look that says, "Where have you been?" Fletcher pulls her into a tight embrace and says nothing.

Saturday morning, 7am, they start. All off-duty police officers and community volunteers gather at the meeting point. Two hundred people are divided into groups and each given an area to search. Today they will be hitting the forest and as many of the surrounding fields as possible – the areas where two bodies have already been found. They will be looking closely for visual signs of bodies, searching under every leaf pile, in every crowded thicket. Other professionals have also been brought in to follow and search for disturbances in the ground, looking for body-shaped disturbances in the earth's magnetic field, looking for changes in soil texture. Unfortunately, despite their knowledge, experience and equipment, Joanna Reagan's remains will stay shrouded in soil just outside the search sites.

One officer irritably jabs a stick into some bushes. He is annoyed, his arms and legs are already covered with itching insect bites. Why am I giving up my weekend for this? I could be playing football, I could be ... his thoughts are interrupted as his stick becomes stuck on something. Great! Another dead animal! Angrily he pulls the bush aside to become face to face with decomposition. A stench of rotting carcass hits his mouth, as he lets out a vomit choked scream before collapsing forward next to the festering body of one former Thomas Goldrick.

They would eventually conclude that Thomas Goldrick died of unknown reasons, his body too badly decomposed for a coroner to determine. His history of heart problems and age lead them to determine that Thomas had become confused on the way home and, despite living in the same area all his life, took the wrong path and wandered lost until the heart attack hit. It is a loose theory, and his widow will eventually accept it.

Down by the river, where nobody goes, there is a small bundle of clothes, a wishy and a washy and a one, two, three... Her screams echo across the forest.

A volunteer has been aiding several officers who are dragging the river. Her job is to catalogue everything they pull out. Throwing discarded bottles and cans into recycling bags, rubbish into rubbish bags. She feels a small sense of pride from just cleaning the river, admiring how nice it looks. Maybe, she thinks, maybe she will bring her children down here, it will be a nice place for a picnic. She smiles with the thought, already seeing her children playing in the trees as her eyes catch sight of a small glimpse of blue – a blanket, hidden under a nearby bush. More abandoned clothes. The blanket feels heavy as she lifts it out from its nesting place. Puzzled, she pulls back the folds and begins to scream. A day-old baby smothered in the blanket. His mother will never be found.

There is a small air of depression, despair and anger as the search groups slowly leave, several volunteers sobbing. One officer will never be able to forget the smell of decomposition. The forest has only given up two sad secrets, neither of them relevant to the actual case. They return the next day, the forest is gloomy and dark. The search continues with sleepless eyes and trembling fingers. The groups are less eager now, the tragedies of the previous day have swatted all enthusiasm. Some people are hoping not to find a body, not to have to see. The searchers are still diligent though, despite aching limbs from the previous day's search, despite itching bug bites. They check as much as they can for hours and hours, but nothing. They stop briefly as food and refreshments are brought out by other volunteers, search for a few hours more before finally giving up and heading home, empty handed to neglected families.

Michaels has been supervising the comings and goings on both days. She has been left at the meeting point alone, with food and water supplies for the group, monitoring the sign-ins and outs. They are calling it a day now, the sun is beginning to dip low in the sky, rain is threatening. The sad search will begin next weekend. Her finger runs down the lists, looking for anyone who hasn't already signed out. 34 – Susanna Hardy.

"This is base calling 34, this is base calling 34."

"34 here."

"Time to come home 34."

"Be ten minutes, base."

"Roger."

57 – Michael Jennings.

55

"This is base calling 57, this is base calling 57."

"Did you say 57?"

"Yes, 57."

"57 here."

"Time to come home, 57."

"Sign me out, base."

"Roger."

133 – Shannon Leona

"This is base calling 133. This is base calling 133."

Static fizzles down the radio, Michaels slaps the walkie-talkie in annoyance.

"This is base calling 133. This is base calling 133."

Silence across the frequency.

"This is base calling 133. Please come in 133."

Silence.

CHAPTER FIVE

F our hundred people take the train into the city every weekday. Most of them sleepwalk in, their eyes half closed in those last throes of slumber. Some use the morning to catch up on paperwork, hurrying through unimportant documents. Some flirt. No one really looks out the window any more, the view never changes. The first train passes within seconds, a chug chug blowing dust over frozen eyes.

The second train passes ten minutes later. One person sees something but isn't quite sure. It is just a trick of the light, the train is going too fast to really see ... but it looks like ... but it isn't ... definitely not. No one else is reacting, was just a trick of light.

It takes five trains before someone alerts the guard, who doesn't really take the teenager seriously, despite the wide-eyed pleading, the I-know-what-I-saw, it was a dead woman! The defiant teenager is met with reassurances and eye rolls from the guard who has heard it all before. The teenager sits back in his seat, arms crossed angrily glaring at the other passengers, protesting that he knows what he saw. No one believes him.

Sixth train, people are more awake now. When one woman screams, the rest of the carriage pay attention. Several people catch the glimpse of flesh and blood as it speeds past their window. Some people say that it is just a prank, a really nasty prank. Others babble incoherently, arriving at work on edge, shaking and babbling until their boss finally sends them home. The nearest station is radioed and a police car is dispatched. At this point no one is really taking the call seriously. It isn't until the order comes through for trains to be diverted, until several cars speed past, their sirens blazing that the realisation hits.

She had been dumped in front of the tunnel, her bloodied head resting against the mossy bricks. Her bruised, clothed body resting at a slant, her cut hand hidden behind her back as if to hide her shame from the cameras, her walkie-talkie still giving off a dying bleep. A female that most of the assembled knew. A female some of them had spent the night searching the forest for, wanting to believe that she had become lost. 133 – Special Constable Shannon Leona.

Shannon Leona had volunteered to become a Special Constable seven years ago. It was how she met her husband Robert Leona, Robbie Bobbie, one of the full-time officers. She worked part-time as a nursery assistant and volunteered part-time with the police force. She did it because she wanted to help the world. She did it because it felt good, the police force felt like family. There had been resentment when she first signed up, the ritual hazing but slowly she was accepted. Her relationship with Robert helped. Shannon would take the Friday night shifts, volunteer to talk down drunk teenagers, never cared when her shoes were vomited on, never scared when someone tried to take a swing. She had a reputation in the force for being able to calm down almost anyone, no matter what the situation.

She would have been horrified to be remembered this way, that her friends had to see her like this. She prided herself on being a strong woman never allowing herself, even at school, to submit to any humiliation. She had been dragged and beaten but she fought as long as she could. Smashing against the cold confines, screaming through a bloody gag, kicking as hard as she could.

In the end, she only amused him. He enjoys reliving that moment when her eyes widened with ... recognition.

Robbie Bobbie was given his nickname by his colleagues, and took it in good part. He took most things with a wide grin. The class clown at school, the class clown at work. Now his eyes are cold and hollow as his partner takes him aside and begins to tell him the news. It takes six colleagues to hold him back, to stop him from running over to the crime scene. He just won't stop struggling and screaming and scratching, half pulling the others across the floor before he finally breaks against the human wall, collapsing into his partner with tears in his eyes.

Robert Leona would never return to work after that day, couldn't stand to see his wife being slowly replaced. Couldn't stand to see the pictures pinned to the board. Couldn't stand to see the colleagues who failed to protect her. Couldn't stand to be a suspect.

They had to bring in another pair of detectives from a different district, Dalbiac and Vogel, these are detectives who had no personal connection to Shannon or Robert Leona. Despite the link to the other victims, this case had to be worked separately. Once the detectives had the unfortunate job of interviewing every officer, every volunteer who had helped with the search, they had to dredge through every workplace conflict involving the Leonas, all those old rivalries and misunderstandings. Poke through any case involving either of the Leonas to try and find any resentful party. They would be there for a long, unwelcomed time.

Fletcher and Bullface have been relieved of all other open cases. Their sole occupation centres on the Numbers murders. Both can feel the pressure mounting, Shannon's murder means that the entire district is watching them, making sure no one slips up, nothing slips away. There is an anger buzzing in the air, the station is a thunderstorm of anger, they had failed to protect so many including one of their own. They were angry at Fletcher and Bullface for not catching this guy yet, angry at each other just for existing, angry at other people's anger. The station is now motivated, powered and fuelled by anger, which is always a catalyst for catastrophe.

Bullface tries to escape from the station as much as possible, taking any opportunity to leave. She feels like the station is smothering her, the same way her first marriage had smothered her in blame and anger. The accusing eyes are haunting her again and she wants out, wants this to be over. Fletcher tries to soothe, he tries to be everyone's friend. He knows that people need to see him working, need a punchbag, need to be reassured that they are actually doing something, but so far the results are disappointing and no one will forgive him for that. Even though they see he is working hard and even though they know it is not his fault. The assailant has managed to pull an entire station apart with one single well-planned murder.

The other detectives are not helping. Interviews by Dalbiac and Vogel have ended with officers storming out, swearing, launching a formal complaint or all three, no one comes out of these interviews smiling. To Fletcher, they seem to be making a bad situation even worse. He was one of the first to be interviewed and had been grilled almost abusively about the lack of progress on the case. While those detectives are there, everyone in the station suspects everyone else, hating and resenting the implication that one of their own could have done that to Shannon Leona.

It's funeral week. Stella McQam is cremated with little ceremony. No family attend, just three of her friends. Unknowingly as they sob, they are watched by waiting cameras. Adelina's funeral is next, closed casket. Adelina's funeral is crowded, the sobbers gathered in close, the chorus of cries echoes from gravestone to gravestone. Jack Sasha stands protectively close to his wife's casket. The fierce anger has faded, his face is a chiselled blank. Jack is accepting the, *"I am sorry – if there is anything I can do."* The handshakes with small nods. He barely notices who is talking to him. This is fortunate for the mousey woman. She approaches Jack with her head fixed on the ground. She has deliberately worn the same dress that she had worn to her daughter's funeral. She has caught a few of the mourners staring at her, trying to figure out who she is. She waits on the outside of the throes, waiting to catch Jack on his own. She knows from her own sad experience, that being alone at the funeral is a rarely given reprieve.

She whispers in his ear, "May I talk to you, Mr Sasha?"

The response is an immediate scowl. "Leave me alone."

"Please, Mr Sasha."

Jack Sasha growls at her.

"I am not a reporter."

"Then who the fuck are you?" Jack glares at the mousey woman.

"My name is Jennifer Taylor."

He doesn't recognise her, why would he? Her daughter's death had not attracted the same amount of attention. She had not appeared on the news threatening revenge. "I am Fran Lizzie Taylor's mother." She says with a hushed whisper.

Anna Stevenson is also at the funeral. She wears carefully selected black strappy heels, ones that Adelina would have approved of. Ones that say, I can be sexy but still sorrowful. Also she wears a skimpy black dress, carefully designed to minimise her flabby gut. Her make-up has been carefully chosen for its waterproof elements and has been slightly reapplied. She is going for it – well she would be, had Jack not walked off with the strange timid woman who had approached him moments before. She and Jack disappear behind another gravestone, much to the astonishment of the other bereaved. Anna is not impressed. Adelina's mother has started wailing again, unhappy that her daughter's husband is already cavorting with another. Anna stares at the red rose and white lily arrangements that surround the cut in the earth. A stone sinks deep within her stomach, it is finally hitting just whose funeral she is attending. For the first time Anna Stevenson feels ashamed of herself, slowly backing away, alone to her car, to collapse in a gooey pile of tears.

Shannon Leona's funeral will be on Friday. Her autopsied body has finally been released. Officers who had attended the search are still under suspicion. Some have even been warned that perhaps they should not attend Shannon's funeral, particularly those who were members of Shannon's search group and the unfortunate officers who had arrived back late.

Fletcher lies in bed, listening to his wife's slightly congested breathing. His eyes are burning, red raw from too many late nights, his whole body throbs in the throes of exhaustion yet he cannot sleep. His mind runs over every single event, trying to find that single elusive clue that he knows they have missed. Should he go out now? Begin a random search alone, the guy could be killing right now, what is he doing lying in bed? If someone died tonight it would be his fault.

But then that's why they employed night staff, who are all vaguely competent, he is only human after all and humans need sleep. Even the killer needs sleep.

Shannon's death hurts, their biggest failure yet. Robert Leona was a good friend; they had been on the same rugby team for eight years. He had attended Robbie's stag do, Robbie laughing his way through the night. It could have been Claire. Playing little juvenile tricks on his fellow officers, forcing them all to dress up as superheroes. His mind plays their wedding over and over. Could have been Claire. The smiling Shannon looking up at Robbie. Could have been Claire. Now Robert won't even talk to him, won't answer the phone, won't return his calls. Robert's message is clear, leave me alone.

Were there more out there? Had he killed Shannon to stop them from getting too close? Her death had brought chaos to the station, no one was willing to revisit the site. Had she stumbled across something? There were victims out there, there had to be. But trying to get another search organised was met with open hostility and anger. Fletcher was not respecting the dead. But then he knew what number had been embedded in Shannon's hand. They didn't. They had found number 2, Jane Doe 217; number 22, Fran Lizzie Taylor; number 28, Stella McQam; unknown number, Adelina Sasha and now, the left hand of Shannon Leona had revealed the number 30.

Sometimes Aaron Fletcher wishes he had chosen a different career, one which allows him to sleep at night without feeling guilty.

Shannon's death had made the news more dramatically than Adelina's. Someone had reminded a certain reporter of Fran Lizzie's death and hinted that maybe all three deaths were connected. Not to be outdone, someone else also reminded them of the death that hadn't even made the news yet – the prostitute Stella McQam. Rumour-mongers were plagued with questions, had Shannon, Adelina and Fran also been posing as working girls? Not to darken the honourable Leona's name, but maybe she had been working undercover? Or over the covers? Had the girls known each other? A secret government connection? The hidden Charlie's angels? These questions were usually met with anger, even from Fran Lizzie's father who used to be a mild-tempered man. Jack Sasha had stopped answering his phone. Steve, Fran's boyfriend left the city and Robert Leona filed harassment charges against anyone who dared to knock on his door, even against those who used to be his co-workers. The shocking aspect of a Special Constable being brutally struck down in the line of duty made even national news. The police station was swamped with calls from the indignant, demanding to know more.

The news coverage means that Shannon Leona cannot be buried peacefully. Her family are torn between honouring her, with a large open funeral that anyone she had known or helped could attend. But this also meant that He could attend, He could try to target someone else there at her funeral. That would be ... too much for some to cope with. The press would be there trying to find a good story, and police force would also be there to keep the peace, neither would be welcome, besides most people would be there just to gape, not to care.

Or maybe they should have a quiet little cremation which only close family could attend. But then would the city forget Shannon? Did her life not deserve to be known and celebrated? Shannon's mother drank a bottle of gin a day during the decision-making battle, Robert Leona started smoking again. No one was coping well. Robert felt conflicted between leaving his wife to suffocate in the dirt or to burn. He had seen her, insisted on seeing her. Didn't want her to spend a minute longer in the morgue, wants her to come home, to be safe. He has heard of cases, of tombstone vandalism, of killers returning to graves and can't face it, can't face him taunting her again. He is torn between tears and anger until finally they decide that she should come home. She will be safer at home. Shannon hated fuss, had always hated fuss, even their wedding was simple. Her dress had been bought on sale, nothing could be flamboyant. Robert knew his wife well, she had never wanted to be a victim and he could not stand her being remembered as one. Finally, they agreed on a small ceremony, allowing the police force to honour the fallen, no cameras, no press, no well-wishers.

Then just as quickly it is over. The phone keeps ringing. Little notes and cards are still pushed through his door. Robert knows they will eventually stop, they will give up and circle the next tragedy. The ashes of his wife are now safe, hidden away from the scavengers. He sits alone in his empty house, his hands clutching a carefully worded note from one Mrs Jennifer Taylor.

CHAPTER SIX

The rumours have twirled into the air and they are everywhere, twisted into every conversation, every thought. Everyone has a theory on who the murderer might be. Everyone has a theory on what he has done to his victims. Although no official police statements have been released, the public are aware that the police are appealing for information on several different murders – murders the rumours insist that are definitely linked. The numbers slashed into hands has so far remained a secret, but everyone knows that the bodies have been mutilated in some way. Some insist that their hearts have been taken, some argue that it was their fingers others say that's absurd, the murderer was definitely taking pieces of their hair. Everyone seems quietly confident that this murderer is definitely a male, perhaps between the ages of twenty to thirty. They speculate that he is a man of a broken home, his wife has probably cheated on him and bled him dry in a bitter divorce. Now, as a result he is an inferno of rage towards women in general. Others scoff at these theories. He is a drug addict killing for jewellery and purses most surely. Some are still convinced that all four women were secret prostitutes and their pimp was wiping them all out, in preparation for fresher meat.

Outright accusations so far have been silent, but the bookies do have a few favourites. The Krill is still the biggest contender, though how he manages to leave his house in the middle of the night unseen is another mystery. The surveillance on his house has been increased, more and more people are trying to see the evil behind the black-out curtains. There are other rumours of course, some think the school's headmaster may be a dark horse. Some parents never quite got the right impression of him, something just not quite right about him, there is something sinister about the smile that hides behind his owlish glasses and that cold clammy handshake. Fat Crack is the two to one shot, since most of the theories involve drugs in some way and where there is drugs, there is Fat Crack. But then how can that mass of disorganised blubber even convince a woman to say hello to him let alone meet him in an abandoned warehouse, field or alleyway? Sometimes those who are pointing fingers rarely consider logic or reason. The main problem though is that people are scared. They are extremely scared. They know for sure there have been at least four women, at least four, there could be more. Every female could be in danger, every male could be a suspect.

The police station has set up special hotlines, one for each of the fallen women, broadcasting appeals for information. Has anyone seen anything suspicious? Anyone with blood-stained clothes? The phones ring and ring, hundreds of calls pounding through the lines, demanding information and attention.

"This is ridiculous, I have kids who want to play in that park!"

"Madam." The patient officer begins wearily.

"Just tell me this! Why haven't you arrested the The Krill yet?"

"Please stop wasting police time."

"You don't understand, The Krill is just a nickname the local kids gave him, I don't know his real name, he lives at ..."

"She tasted so good ... I think you would taste good too, Officer." The officer is momentarily stunned as the prank caller gives a wild giggle then hangs up the phone.

No one really has any useful information. Fletcher and Bullface have had more officers added to their team, they are useless as far as Bullface is concerned. The officers are reviewing every little detail of each case again, Bullface doubts they will find anything worth the overtime. The search for Adelina's elusive jogger friend continues. Fran Lizzie had not complained of anyone stalking or threatening her. Fran's case is hard, no one suspicious had been acting strangely nearby. No one had seen her leave with anyone. They had nothing to search for. Jane Doe 217 was the hardest, the bones belonging to victim number two could not even yield a name. Not enough teeth for dental records, no DNA match, no family concerned, no one ringing her helpline number. Bullface is angry that they could not even find a name for her, angrier that they can't find any evidence. The only thing that they know is that this is proof the killer has been operating, undetected, for anything up to five years. To Bullface this is unforgivable, twenty-five other victims, still hidden out there but no one willing to search.

Stella's friends had provided little information, Stella saw a lot of different men, yes, some rough ones, yes, but it was all eyes down, no questions asked. The friends have promised to report any threatening men to them, but Bullface doubts they will, they can't afford to hurt their custom. Most of the police force has been cleared now, but the air of suspicion and anger is still deep at the station. It will be a long, long time before officers start trusting each other again.

They seem to be following all the wrong leads, Fletcher decides grimly. It still must be done, they have to exhaust every possibility, every testimony. Exhaust everything so that nothing can come back in court, nothing can be brought up to establish plausible doubt. Even if that means tracking down every single suspect, knocking on every door within a radius of each of the murder sites, of each of the victim's homes, each of the victim's places of work. It takes days and months and more days. September has faded into October and so far no arrests. Fletcher knows they will find nothing now. There is nothing now.

They still have a few leads but he just doesn't see them going anywhere, the more credible leads have been exhausted and those remaining leads are just … petty. Fletcher does not even want to listen to the tips hotline anymore. That job is saved for whoever has been annoying him lately. It is just blank time, the long wait in the game, he knows the killer won't strike just yet, there is too much paranoia, not even Brad fucking Pitt can convince a woman to go anywhere alone with him at this point. Too many people are watching, waiting for him and he knows it. In order to try and control the paranoia and panic, to reduce the number of scared, tearful phone calls, in order to reassure the public, more police cars have been brought onto the streets. Overtime has become mandatory but now there is just too much police presence on the streets. They have reduced the chance of there being more victims at the expense of actually catching this fucker. Fletcher's head is a permanent throbbing mass, always tense with worry. He constantly grinds his teeth. There is a little positive outcome, the police's stronger presence on the streets has meant they have caught three burglars, one would-be rapist and a drunk who is still insisting he has a right to visit his kids no matter what the judge says. But not the killer, he still remains in the shadows, a permanent threat to Claire and every other woman out there.

Brandi Parr is almost enjoying the workplace paranoia. Marcella has turned into a snivelling blob, whining to anyone who comes near about how afraid she is, how unsupportive her boyfriend is being. People are beginning to come up to Brandi now, making sure that she is OK. They are actually concerned about her, Brandi, the office weirdo. No longer are they making jokes about her parents being alcoholics or anything stupid to do with her name (Randy Brandi being the worst of the jokes). But now they are actually concerned. All the single females in the office are being given special treatment, they are making sure no one has to go home alone. Marcella's near emotional breakdowns mean that the office is tip-toeing around them, trying oh so hard not to upset the potential victims any more. The quite cute intern Mike Jones has shown particular interest in Brandi's safety, offering to escort her anywhere. Much of the conversation in the office centres around the tragedy of that poor police officer, brought down so young. How those girls just didn't deserve to die, in death their every flaw is gone. No one talks about Stella as a prostitute, instead they say she was a pretty young woman who didn't deserve to die. Brandi is enjoying the debates over a possible murderer, enjoying the rumours surrounding The Krill, enjoying gossiping about rumours no one believes to be true. Suddenly her tame life isn't so dull. She almost hopes they will never catch this guy.

Elizabeth Mitchell is also enjoying herself, in a way. Watching out for him has given her something to do. It is more exciting than watching her soaps day in and out (although they are still playing softly in the background). She is planning an attack. She has been watching the house for weeks now and thinks she knows his schedule. She has the spare key that Old Arnie had given her before he died. The man living in Old Arnie's house hasn't appeared to have changed the locks or even put in a security system. Evil doesn't fear evil is what her mother used to say. Elizabeth decides that she will enter the house, when he has gone. Miss Marple meets Mrs Mitchell. Super sleuth. She will go in and look for more evidence. Since the police aren't doing anything, she will have to. She hadn't trusted him, right from the moment he had moved in. The devil's music blasts through the air, interrupting her thoughts. His rusty car slams to a stop and then he climbs out. Right on schedule, Elizabeth ducks behind the curtain to make another note on her clipboard with a small amount of glee. She is going to get him, she is going to get him. Can hide from the police, may think you are free, but you can't hide from me, she sings to herself softly.

October becomes November with little celebration. There have been no more murders, the city is beginning to settle down, but Bullface doubts that this killer is finished. The police station is still working in stern determination, they have to find this guy no matter what. Has he moved away? Some families have, with a *"if a special constable isn't safe then who is"* attitude. They have loaded up and moved away, staying with relatives until their houses are sold. Has he moved with them? Following a specific target? It is possible, they are trying to keep the other stations informed, the computers have helped here. If a crime is committed in certain areas of the world, with the DNA matching the DNA found at the four different dump sites then they will be informed, Bullface hopes. Not that they actually had the perpetrator's DNA. They have one hundred and ten different pieces of evidence with DNA on it, taken from four different crime scenes. All because he was killing in open areas, well-littered open areas, well-littered open areas that were just filled with DNA samples. Forty of these samples were female and so were considered to be very unlikely, that left seventy pieces. Maybe the perpetrator is one of them. Four of those pieces have been in the system for prior offences but the alibis had checked out. Hundreds of hours of police work have drawn up and then disqualified every possible lead – elusive bastard!

Bullface has unconsciously been crunching her teeth at night from the frustration, much to her husband's annoyance. At home, she has broken a coffee table with one frustrated kick. But here in the police station, she is trying to keep her exterior calm. Fletcher will never know just how close he had come to a swift kick in the ... area. Fletcher is annoying her because he has been too restrained, too quiet and thoughtful, something is definitely going on in his head. Bullface deepens her scowl, what is her partner keeping from her? She doesn't want to think about it but can't stop thinking about it, she turns to hack away at the fort of papers on her desk. She isn't leaving today until her desk is clear, she had promised herself this earlier.

November 11th, 12.18am

The bag is slowly unzipped, strong hands gently pull her out of the bag and place her on the cold metal table. The room is completely silent, with only the faint noise of traffic intruding through the blacked-out windows. Methodically she is stripped and then the coroner leans over her with slight astonishment.

The night had been cold, whispers of snow tracing the air. When they found her she had stared up at the two baffled police officers and they had stared down. Shivering, they stood over her corpse, not knowing what to make of it all. The number on the left hand is understood all too well but not this ... other stuff. The dance began around her, the hours of patient photographing, documenting and orders were given. Then she was brought here, for answers.

"Victim's right leg, calf area. What appears to be a butterfly has been drawn on the victim's leg. This has been drawn on in felt tip pen, using the colours red, blue, black and yellow."

One assistant scribbles frantically, another assistant documents each drawing with several photographs. A bright-green alien waves to the assistants from the right thigh. A yellow and pink striped rose takes up most of the left leg. The victim's right arm holds a rainbow, two more butterflies and an apple, while her left arm inexplicably depicts a pink and purple dinosaur. A wasp buzzes around the victim's neck, drawn in a bright yellow and black, stained with a darkening red.

Cause of death was a knife wound to the throat, death instantaneous.

"It is the same MO as Fran Lizzie's," Bullface states, staring down at the blood-stained street. "Throat was slit, no defensive wounds, no sexual assault. She didn't see it coming."

"Any ID?"

"Nope, victim's purse was taken. She was found next to an abandoned shopping bag, I sent an officer to see if the clerk can tell us anything." She pauses. "The bag contained a bottle of Fairy Liquid, Stardust, two bags of lollipops and a bag of toffee popcorn."

"Munchies?" Fletcher's lips move as he is thinking.

"Possibly." Little humour ever passes Bullface's lips. "She was covered in drawings."

Fletcher pauses, not quite knowing what to say. "Drawings?" he manages weakly.

"Felt-tipped all over her body."

"Do you think the assailant..." A pause while Fletcher tries to figure out a sensitive way to phrase this.

"It's a possibility but not a likely one," she mutters. "Trauma to the left hand again."

Fletcher's heart sinks, shit shit shit his mind is already chanting.

"Did anyone else see?"

"We are not sure."

"Who found her?"

"Anonymous tipster. Have got Smith and Seasions checking out the call location, Juda and Hendy seizing all available CCTV."

There is just one last question to ask, the question that breaks their familiar routine. "What number was she?" he asks, not actually wanting to hear the answer.

Bullface murmurs a reply.

Oh shit shit shit.

That number rings in his head over and over. Fletcher just wants to go home, grab Claire and leave the city. Go as far away as possible, the other end of the country, another country, a place where no one has to face monsters. This is his first instinct. However, Fletcher is still a police officer, still sworn to protect the peace and while every nerve in his body is on edge, whispering that they should get out of here, go where it is safe, his mind tells him to get a grip. Officers of the law don't just run away when it gets too hard, whispers a voice that sounds questionably like his father-in-law. Officers don't leave innocents to suffer, get a fucking grip, man. This is the second time he has wanted to go home rather than work a case this year, maybe he just isn't cut out to be a police officer anymore. Hell, he has been one for the last ten years of his life, it's all he wanted to be when he was younger. But maybe, maybe he has made a mistake. Then it isn't like he can just turn round to Bullface and say, sorry old bird, but I can't do this anymore. I am just going to go home like a good castrato and drink cocoa until all this nasty malarkey blows over. No he can't do anything like that. He owes it to Shannon, to all of these women to keep going. Maybe, though, maybe just maybe, he will suggest to Claire that she should be the one who leaves the city. He will be able to handle this better, he reassures himself, once he knows that Claire is safe. Oh shit though, they are now up to victim number 34.

Bullface is annoyed. She is usually annoyed but now she is verging from annoyed onto inferno angry. The perpetrator has taken every opportunity he can to torment them, to slow them down. He took the victim's purse, and with it, he took the easiest way to identity the victim. They will have to wait until someone reports her as missing. It slows them down, means that maybe a trail or two will go cold before they can even ID her. If they can ID her! They already have over two hundred sets of unclaimed and unnamed Jane Does in the morgue, all from the last fifty years. Fletcher isn't exactly helping either. Instead, it is her who is issuing orders, collecting evidence while he stands there, looking helpless. She feels like giving him a sharp slap across the face, she is getting violent again. This is not good. Deep breaths, deep breaths, deep fucking breaths, hold in the frustrated screams.

"Hello?" The drunken voice slurs down the phone, the officer grimaces in disgust. He hates working the night shifts, always gets the drunk calls, particularly at one in the morning.

"Iss thiss the police?"

"Yes, do you have a crime to report?" the officer mutters rudely, through gritted teeth.

"My housseemate. She hasn't come back yet. She sup-supposssed to be baack by now,"

The officer can hear someone else yelling in the background, then the drunk voice telling the other to shut the fuck up.

"She went out like two hours ago maybe. She was a wee bit pissed, she was."

"Sir, this isn't a police matter."

"Just wanted ya to keep an eye out for her."

"OK, what is your friend's name?" It is easier to take a description than to argue with the drunk, the officer decides.

"Izzzie."

"OK, what does she look like?" Maybe he will send a squad car over tomorrow, frighten the prat, give him the standard don't waste police time lecture.

"She's pretty."

"OK." Definitely send over a car.

"She drew all over herself. Ya would notice."

"She drew all over herself?" he says in slight astonishment.

One of the other officers looks over sharply.

"Ya, like Wasspssss, ya?"

The house is a mess, not just a mess it could be used as a dictionary definition for disorganisation. Fletcher and Bullface cautiously walk into the kitchen, trying their hardest not to step on anything too ... gooey. The kitchen itself is painted a painfully bright yellow, with matching orange cupboards. The work stations are covered in dirty dishes, empty vodka bottles, scattered playing cards and several suspiciously bright stains. Leading out of the kitchen, Fletcher can see another door, covered in brightly drawn images of dragons, robots, rabbits and what looks like a cheese grater. A bright plaque proudly proclaims that this room belonged to *Sir Izz the Mad*, Isobel's room.

One of the piles in the kitchen groans, startling them both, Bullface is the first to realise that the pile is actually a person, they watch in stunned silence as the pile slowly tries to stand up, fails, tries again and then passes out again, falling heavily to the floor.

"Don't mind him, he's a lightweight he is." Their tour guide, Frank, isn't completely sober either, his girlfriend's death hasn't quite penetrated through the warm alcoholic buzz.

"So." He isn't quite sure what to do with his unexpected guests, the man on the phone said they needed to ask him some questions. He hopes Izzie will be home soon, she is better at answering questions than he is. He had hoped they had found her and were bringing her back. The only reason he answered the door was because he thought it might be her. Where was Izzie?

"Is there anyone we can call for you?" Fletcher asks softly.

Frank's eyes light up and he smirks dreamily. "Pizza?"

Fletcher and Bullface exchange sharp glances. There be no easy way of saying this.

November 11th, 2.32am

He slowly slides through the open window, trying hard not to cause any creaks, then slides down into the living room. Photographs of a smiling family glare at him from the wall. He pulls the window close, not wanting the neighbours to see, then tiptoes across the cool wooden floor. He pulls off his shoes at the living room door as silently as possible. There are young children in this house, which means the huge possibility that there are toys still on the floor. He will have to be very careful. He slides his feet forward, first one foot, then another. He leaves the living room door open, not wanting to cause any unnecessary sound. They should all be in a deep sleep by now, but he isn't going to take any chances. He moves forward into the hall. It isn't so dark here. But it is silent and eerie, he likes this time of night, so calm and quiet. He begins to slowly climb the stairs, his heart palpitating wildly from the strain, his mouth feels dry. He feels almost giddy and light-headed. Just a few more steps. He slides onto the landing, so far so good. A smile spreads across his face. His hands grip the master bedroom door, slowly creaking it open.

CRAAAACK.

He mutters a soft oomph then collapses onto the carpeted floor. His wife of ten years stands over him, still brandishing a golf club, her eyes wild with fear, arms shaking with adrenaline. He will never regain consciousness.

"I thought he was the killer." The wife sobs over and over again, crying into court rooms and cameras.

November 11th, 2.45am

Kain wakes up. Coughs briefly then checks the stairs before going back to sleep.

November 11th, 1.34pm

The word on the street is that there had been two murders last night. Offices are again buzzing with rumours. The word has been spread by neighbours that police cars and ambulances had been visiting in the night. So many had heard the screams of the devastated wife, was he attacking families now? It has only been two months since the last murders. He is working fast! Panic rushes through all the rumours, some people leave work early then just leave the city without even going home first.

She types frantically at her desk with quivering hands, not noticing just how many words she is misspelling. It could be you next. It could be you next. It could be ... is the mantra repeating over and over in her head, He is attacking families now, he is attacking families, could be you, over and over as she tries to concentrate on her work. Her boss says her name softly and she looks over at him sharply, her eyes glazed with tears.

"I am not going to risk my family," she screams loudly at him, her hands grabbing frantically at her purse before turning and half running, half stumbling out the door. Her poor confused boss repeating over and over to anyone who would listen that he had only asked her to make a photocopy.

The police call lines are extremely busy, please hold all our operators are currently on a call, please hold. They keep adding more staff, more volunteers but it is never enough. They can't keep up with the incoming calls, as fresh appeals for information are broadcast, looking desperately for the last people to see Isobel Hilarie aka Izzie aka Izz the Mad alive.

Isobel's university vice-chancellor has issued a statement on the loss of their promising art student, the university will be shut for the rest of the day, out of respect. They will also increase campus security (again) and are considering enforcing a curfew. The vice-chancellor doesn't mention how drunk Izzie had been the night before, doesn't mention that after drawing on herself for several hours she decided that she was hungry and set forth on a brave quest for food. Her love for quests, dragons and fantasies is not mentioned nor does anyone say she was basically a kid in an adult's body, which is why she named herself Sir Izz the Mad. She is just a victim now, no longer a person.

Madison Albrook has decided not to waste her unexpected day off, sure she has other things she should be doing but she is still going to use this time wisely and effectively. She isn't going to do her coursework or the small mound of washing that now covers most of her floor. Instead she is going to do something she has been putting off for a while now. Something she has wanted to do since she came to university and got away from her mother's hawk eyes. She is going to get her clitoris pierced. She thinks it will make an amazing story to frighten her grandchildren with one day. Also it will scare the beeswax out of Mrs Chalmers, the old lady in the flat below, the lady who opens her door every time Madison leaves her flat. Always to ask Madison, "What are you doing to protect yourself from this monster? You must take more care, my dear. Would you like me to get Augustus to escort you?"

Madison knows that this is all a pretence. Mrs Chalmers's thirty-year-old son Augustus has a crush on her, and he has made the ultimate mistake of admitting so to his mother. Now the old bat just won't stop trying to push them together, refusing to believe that Madison does not want to go out with a man ten years older, a man who stinks of sweat and cat pee.

Gleefully she tells Mrs Chalmers exactly where she is going and hopes the look of disgust she receives means Mrs Chalmers will stop trying to hook her up with her darling Augustus. It is turning out to be a good day, despite that girl's death.

She is excited, she is going to do something daring! Something her mother would forbid. She smiles to herself, something that could be easily undone if she doesn't like it. This is a start to all the daring things she told herself she would do once she was free, a start to a new her.

Unfortunately the only people who ever got to see her brand new piercing were the overworked coroner and his assistants. They were only a little shocked. They have seen worse, much worse.

November 11th, 3.05pm

Madison Albrook's body is found, face down in a sea of blood-red memorial poppies. She lies dead centre in the display. This image will scream across the front page of every newspaper the following day. What doesn't make the papers is the number 36 felt-tipped across her right hand.

Fletcher had gone home at 2am, they had spent well over an hour talking to Frank, Izz's boyfriend. Or rather, trying to talk to him. For a long time it was impossible to even get through to him, Fletcher suspected the man returned to drinking the moment they left. Frank is now a man who will never want to sober up.

Fletcher had wearily hit the bed, closed his eyes and slept until a piercing shrill shook through him, breaking through the exhausted sleep. His eyes slowly opened, his mind unable to grasp that buzzing sound, the insistent squeal, echoing. His hand clumsily reaches out, banging down hard on the snooze button. The buzzing continues, it isn't the alarm clock. Finally he realises it is the phone and that he has overslept, really overslept.

"Hello?"

"We need you in, there has been another one."

"I'll be thirty minutes."

Bullface hangs up without even as a much as a goodbye.

Fletcher quickly showers, pulling on his favourite green jumper. He likes the way he looks in this green jumper, to him it says *'Yes, I am an officer, I am looking pretty sharp but you can still trust me!'* He admires the way it fits over and hides the slight puffs of his abdomen, it is a good jumper he decides. Even its familiar sweet smell of laundry detergent and cookies comforts him. Everyone who sees him today, won't be able to take their eyes off that green offender, wondering what had possessed the man to buy such an ugly jumper. Fletcher tries to keep his thoughts and feelings focused completely on the jumper, trying hard not to think. Where is Claire? Is it her this time? No, no, Bullface would have told him, then again she might not know. No, no, Claire would be at work, there is no reason it could be her. There is every reason it could be her. Fletcher's fingers hover anxiously on his mobile, there is no harm in just checking, right? Under the pretence of telling her he will be late home again. Depression slinks back in, the green jumper just isn't as comforting as it used to be.

Florescent lights glare accusingly above Bullface. The room is silent apart from the chorus of office sounds breaking through only when someone softly opens the door and solemnly takes a seat. Bullface does not turn around to meet them nor even acknowledge them. Instead she continues to write on the board in front on them. Neatly, carefully printing every damned word. The computer next to her projects a screen-saver on the awaiting screen.

2. *Jane Doe 217 (Deceased between two to five years)*
   Age 17–25 (estimated)
   Trauma to the left hand
   C.O.D – Unknown

22. *Fran Lizzie Taylor (March 9th)*
    Age 22 (and 22 days)
    Number inflicted on left hand
    C.O.D – Throat cut

Number Not Known – Adelina Sasha (August 21st)
   Age 38
   Trauma to the left hand
   C.O.D – Throat cut
   Trauma inflicted to face, stomach and arms

28. *Stella McQam (August 24th)*
    Age 37
    Number inflicted on right hand
    C.O.D – Stab to the heart

30. *Shannon Leona (August 30th)*
    Age 29
    Number inflicted on left hand.
    C.O.D – Exsanguination
    Trauma inflicted across the body

Here her writing becomes heavy, she presses down too sharply on her marker pen, willing it to break in her hand. Only creating a squeak that makes the other members in the room look up sharply.

34. Isobel Hilarie (November 11th)
Age 19
Number inflicted on left hand
C.O.D – Throat cut

36. Madison Albrook (November 11th)
Age 20
Number drawn on right hand
C.O.D – Throat cut

"Shall we begin?" She asks quietly to the assembled room, checking for any missing or unwelcome faces. But where to begin? All of the assembled have been briefed before, everything she knows about the first few deaths, they already know. But now they have two more. Start from the beginning she tells herself but what is even the beginning?

"This morning, the body of Isobel Hilarie was found. She had been dumped on a quiet street." She clicks the computer, projecting the image onto the screen. The assembled detectives see a young girl with dyed purple hair, lying down on the grey pavement, haloed in red. Despite the cold weather she is wearing a short purple top and a bright-blue skirt. The multi-coloured drawings can clearly be seen on her revealed skin.

"The drawings are self-inflicted," Bullface says, knowing that someone is about to ask. "High levels of alcohol were found in her blood. The victim's boyfriend said she had left to buy food, the cashier confirmed seeing her at 10.49pm, which is ten minutes before that store closed. The area she was found in was on her route home." She pauses, allowing the officers time to scribble down the details. "This was not a usual pattern for her, the assailant may not have been targeting her specifically. It is possible he noticed her going into the store and then waited for her to come out."

"Do you think he was waiting in that particular area?"

"It is possible. We don't know anything for certain at the moment. I have two officers going through the CCTV footage for both attacks. See if anyone was caught waiting around or for matches to the footage from the other attacks. Madison Albrook was killed and placed in a very busy area, there is a high chance that he has been caught on camera."

Murmurs drift across the room.

Bullface waits, glaring at them to be quiet.

"Who found Isobel Hilarie?"

"Someone called in from a nearby pay phone. I have the message here." With the image of the fallen Isobel still on the screen, she presses play and the message blares through.

"999, What's your emergency?"

Silence.

"Caller? What's your emergency?"

"There's a girl lying on the pavement. I think she is hurt." The voice is calm. Barely above a whisper. The line is crackly, making the voice barely audible.

"Is she bleeding?" The caller ID has picked up the area, Dispatch is already issuing an unneeded ambulance and squad car.

"Yes."

"Is she still breathing?"

The caller answers by disconnecting the line.

End of recording, silence in the conference room.

"The victim was lying in full view of the phone box," Bullface explains quickly. "Dispatch sent an ambulance to the telephone's location, that's when they found Isobel. I have had an investigation team process the pay phone. She was still warm when they found her. Coroner estimates that he called as she was dying."

"That's a little sloppy."

The glares force the speaker to elaborate.

"The ambulance may have been able to revive her."

"It could be more of a taunt than being careless."

Bullface decides it is best to ignore them and continue with the briefing.

"Madison Albrook is different." She loads the next image on screen. The photo of the twenty-year-old criminology student is artistic in a sickening way, the photo has captured Madison surrounded by a sea of memorial poppies. Face down so no one can see the ugly slit across her neck. Her light blonde hair obscures her face completely. Madison had been wearing dark black jeans and a dark-grey sweater, contrasting harshly with the bright poppies.

"As you can see, she was dumped in the middle of Westgate's Parks Memorial Gardens. Her throat was cut in a similar fashion to Isobel Hilarie, Adelina Sasha and Fran Taylor. But as you can see here, her number was not cut into her hand. Instead the killer used a felt tip marker. Now," Bullface hurries before anyone can get a question in, "there are a number of possibilities. This is a busy park, even in November, particularly because it was Remembrance Day. Madison was found within an estimated ten minutes of her death. There is a possibility he switched to felt tip for this kill because he knew he would not have the time to carve the number in. This would mean that this murder was premeditated, he had chosen the park and waited for the right victim. Other possibilities include the most obvious, that this is a copycat, although the mutilations on the previous murders were not released to the press officially, perhaps word has leaked." Bullface feels tired, very tired, her face a heavy mass of worry and anger. She didn't go to bed until 3am and her husband accidentally woke her at 7. Bullface is fighting the urge to drop, drop right there in the conference room, or to yell at one of the less senior officers present, *"You, you have disrespected me since you arrived here, how about you do my job for a while. Huh? See how well you can do this."* She swallows quickly, trying to bury the tension before continuing in her dry dull tone.

"However, the number inflicted on Madison Albrook continues in the sequence, if this was a copycat, it would have had to have been a lucky guess to get the number right. Or one of our earlier theories included a possibility that the assailant has a partner due to the inconsistency in the kills, the difference between Madison's and Isobel's death could also imply this."

"What kind of inconsistencies?"

Bullface hated when they didn't do the pre-reading.

"As you can see from this," Bullface gestures to the written board, "Stella McQam's number was carved in to the right hand, so was Madison Albrook's, whereas all the other victims had their numbers carved into the left hand. This could indicate a second killer if this is deliberate. Stella McQam was stabbed in the heart whereas the other victims had their throats cut."

Bullface hates herself right here, right now for being able to talk about the victims in such a way. She doesn't see them as humans anymore, they are just victims.

"I know we are tiptoeing around Shannon Leona's death but ..." It seems like a crime to say Shannon Leona's name out loud. No one wants her to be called a victim. "Both Shannon and Adelina had been stabbed repeatedly whereas the other victims were unmarked. This indicates that the killer went into a frenzy with these two women but not the other victims. Maybe an individual factor about these particular victims prompted this or maybe it was because with the other victims he ... they had less time."

"So you think there could be two of them?"

"Right now, there is no evidence to suggest there is just one killer or that there are two or even three killers. We need to consider all possibilities."

"Have you researched into the victimology?"

"So far we cannot find a connection between the victims, they all vary in appearance, age, profession and hobbies. His youngest victim was nineteen, his oldest has been thirty-eight. None of them shared similar facial structures, hair styles or colours."

Bullface has the victim's profile pictures on screen now, flipping through them slowly. First comes the artist's facial reconstruction of Jane Doe 217, then a blurred close up of Jane Doe's face, taken from the only photo they had. Jane Doe had long black hair and evident bruising across her face. Then the picture of Fran Lizzie, a young girl with short brown hair and big green earrings. Then the older Adelina Sasha, still a striking face with long brown hair and green eyes. Stella McQam scowled at the room, from a photograph taken by the police, an ugly figure with false dyed blonde hair and sharp cheekbones. A flash of ginger hair as Bullface quickly shows Shannon Leona's face to the flinching officers. Isobel is a smiling crazed contrast, pulling a face into the camera. Then the serious face of Madison Albrook stalks into view, the picture had been taken of her studying, glancing down at a book through thick glasses.

"Visibly, these women have nothing in common, both Shannon and Madison wore glasses, Fran Lizzie wore contacts. The victims Jane Doe and Adelina Sasha show that he is not sticking to one race either. All these victims had different jobs, Fran Taylor worked as a sales assistant, Adelina Sasha was an office clerk, Stella McQam was a prostitute, Shannon Leona…" Her voice drops slightly. "Isobel Hilarie was a first year art student and Madison Albrook was a second year criminology student. Though they studied at the same university, so far they appear to have no other connecting factors. The assailant may not have even known that they were students. None of the victims lived in similar areas or were members of the clubs or societies. The only thing that these victims have in common is that they are all female. I would also like to mention here, that so far every single one of these victims have had the contents of their purses taken. Since the credit cards have not been used, I believe he is taking these items as trophies. It is possible that when we arrest the assailant that he may have these items in his house or nearby. He has also taken photos of a least one of his kills, maybe more. Anyone searching a house of a suspect should look for these items.

"I think we are looking at an assailant or assailants who kill when the opportunity arises. They don't pick a victim but rather they pick a location, the dump sites have been mostly isolated areas implying the assailant has knowledge of the area. These victims were just in the wrong place at this time."

She pauses, taking a sip of water, allowing a brief moment for questions. The officers continue to scribble furiously at their notes, no one so far is challenging her. She wants to be challenged, she wants a chance to strike.

"The other factor that ties these victims together is that they have all had a number engraved or written on their hand. The most likely conclusion is that the assailant is numbering each of his victims, but then that would also imply that in the space of one day he has killed at least three more victims. Since Isobel Hilarie was number thirty-four and Madison Albrook was number thirty-six, it could imply that there is also a number thirty-five out there. Since victim number twenty-two Fran

Taylor was killed in March, it would also imply that in a space of nine months, twelve victims have been claimed and we have only found six."

"Twelve victims in nine months?"

"It is not that unbelievable. Steve Wright, the Ipswich killer killed five women in three months. Gary Ridgway, the Green River Killer was suspected of killing over ninety victims in sixteen years. Ted Bundy was suspected of killing over thirty-five victims in four years. John Wayne Gacy was convicted of killing thirty-three men in six years. Jack the Ripper is suspected of killing eight prostitutes in under a year and may have continued operating without our knowledge. Richard Chase killed six victims in under a year. Harold Shipman killed over two hundred victims in twenty-three years. If he was working with a partner then maybe that would be a little more credible, but we can't underestimate this assailant." She pauses, not wanting to say this. "He was able to lure away a special constable, in an area surrounded by our volunteers with no one noticing."

There is a hiss of displeasure, more heads bow down not wanting to meet Bullface's eyes.

She continues. "We may not be looking at twelve victims or thirty-six victims but we cannot assume otherwise. Serial killers don't stick to rules or regulations. They are driven by something that not one of us can comprehend. It is possible that he has increased his kills and that he has now killed thirty-six victims but then it is still possible that he is using some kind of code and there have only been six victims so far. Without any other evidence, we cannot assume anything or underestimate just what he is capable of.

"What we do know is that he has killed two victims in less than forty-eight hours before, as Adelina Sasha was killed on August the 21st and Stella McQam on the 24th, now he has killed two victims in less than twenty-four hours. Something is making him speed up. These kills are well planned and well executed so it unlikely that he is devolving. I think we can expect for him to continue at this pace and he won't stop until he is caught."

CHAPTER SEVEN

"There's something you should see." Fletcher stands over Bullface's near-pristine desk. He had given her ten minutes after the meeting to breathe before daring to venture over. He knows that meeting did not go spectacularly well, he could tell by the downcast pessimistic faces that had followed her out. Bullface, well she is called Bullface for a reason, her face is always impassive and stony but Fletcher knows the truth. At least he thinks he knows the truth, Bullface will never be one for a heart-to-heart chat.

She looks up at him, her eyes staring him down making Fletcher feel like a naughty schoolboy. "It's the CCTV footage, we have managed to capture..." He doesn't need to say any more, a small smile may have traced Bullface's lips as she stands and follows him out the room.

The camera had been purposely positioned at the memorial display. The city had suffered severe vandalism the year before and was aiming to tackle it. Bullface watches the grainy footage, watches as a young couple come on screen, she is clutching his arm as if afraid or unable to support herself. They had appeared out of the bushes from the other side of the screen, the male purposely keeps his head down, he is dressed in a dark outfit and is wearing a dark beanie. They are a dark black mass moving across the screen, the camera does not capture his face. Bullface realises with sudden horror that the girl's throat has already been cut. In a matter of seconds, he throws her face down into the poppies. She does not move. The man keeps walking. The screen stays on the image of Madison Albrook, lying awkwardly in the poppies, four minutes go by, no movement. Seven minutes later a second couple appear on screen, their mouths opening in shock, the male goes over to shake Madison, then he freezes. His partner screams silently into the camera. Bullface doesn't care to watch any more.

"This is useless," she mutters.

"It's a start, we might be able to clean the image up."

"It's winter, there are hundreds of men wandering around in black clothes and beanies. We can't make beanies illegal." Out of sight, her hand clenches angrily. "Has he been sighted anywhere else?"

"We are still looking, now we know how he was dressed, he might be easier to spot. I sent a team back to the park, to check if anything was left in those bushes."

"Why didn't they check before?"

"Well, we didn't know before," Fletcher says.

"There should have been a blood trail."

Fletcher is silent.

The couple who found Madison Albrook are still in shock. They sit together, not speaking, hands tightly clasped on top of the cold metal table. The male's eyes are firmly fixed to the cooling coffee in front of him, occasionally his gaze will shift uncomfortably back to his fingers, staring hard as if he could still see the unwelcome droplets of blood. Fletcher reckons they are both around fifty, beginning to lose that battle to old age and frailty. The female stares disapprovingly at the two-way mirror, unknowingly meeting Fletcher's gaze. Her face is stern and cold, reminding him of Bullface. Right now, he doesn't want to be reminded of Bullface, she is most displeased, yes, the last crime scene had not been processed properly. It seems so obvious now, why had no one followed the blood trail? Mistakes have been made, they are only human yes, but this is not a case that can allow any mistakes. If only he wasn't so fucking tired ... Fletcher knows Bullface probably blames him, for not checking the scene properly, for not realising sooner. She had trusted him to run the scene alone while she briefed the other officers and now ... now she knows what a worthless ... no, there is no point in thinking about that now. Fletcher is still in charge of conducting the interviews, still trusted. The pressure has tripled now, this has to go well. No more mistakes will be allowed. First things first before he goes into the room, how does he want the interview to go? He needs to know the right questions to ask, have them ready in his mind, his face needs to be compassionate everything needs to be right to get the best answers.

He knows they are innocent, that's always a good start, the CCTV footage has cleared the couple of any involvement in the attack. Fletcher has already followed them through various parts of the park on the footage and is satisfied that they are innocent. Since these eyewitnesses are not under suspicion he does not need to be seen as a fierce figure of the law. Fletcher has spent months researching different interview techniques, it is his specialism. He knows that if the interviewer speaks in authoritative tones, he will establish control over the eyewitness, meaning they will play a more passive role by providing information they think he wants. Whereas, if he speaks in a more relaxed tone, then they will consider him in a more friendly way ... hopefully, encouraging them to play a more active role, more willing to provide information. But then again as they are an older couple, they may not take him seriously if he is too friendly. Slowly he opens the door.

"Hello, I am Detective Sergeant Aaron Fletcher, how are you both?" he asks politely. The woman gives him a disapproving stare, the man barely notices his arrival.

"We want to go home," the woman says sternly but protectively.

"Well I just have a few questions for you, and then you will be free to leave." The man nods gently, the woman shifts uncomfortably in her seat. It is very clear who in this couple is the dominant personality.

"Let's start at the beginning, what time did you arrive at the park today?" Fletcher tries to keep his tone neutral and open, the woman is still staring at him sullenly.

"We arrived at around two thirty maybe," the man mutters, his eyes still fixated with horror on his hands.

"I would like to do a memory exercise with you, to help you remember this afternoon a little easier."

The woman becomes indignant. "Young man, I assure you there is nothing wrong with our memories."

"Please humour me, madam."

There is silence, though the woman is still visibly bristling. Fletcher wonders idly again, whether she is related to Bullface.

"Please describe the park when you first arrived."

"In what way?" the man says, resignedly.

"What could you see when you first arrived?"

"The park," the woman mutters, still angry at the time-wasting exercise.

"We went to the bird cages first, near the ponds." The man's eyes close tiredly. Fletcher knows just how he feels.

"Did you see anyone near the bird cages?"

"There was a young boy, drawing the birds."

"Can you describe him?"

"I didn't really look at him, he was very young."

"And he was in the park on his own?"

"No, his mother was watching him, she was sitting in the picnic area."

Fletcher slowly writes this information down, allowing them time to elaborate further.

"His mother, what did she look like?"

"She was wearing a purple jumper."

"No it was red," his wife insists.

"Purply-red." He tries to compromise.

"Red."

"What was her hair colour?"

"Brown." The woman insists. The man gives no argument. Maybe this interview would have been more successful if they were interviewed separately. Damn, another mistake.

"What colour top was the boy wearing?"

"Brown, it was a sweater, there was a logo on the front of it."

Fletcher gives the man time to argue before continuing.

"Was he wearing glasses?"

"No, does this really matter?"

"Every detail is important."

"Please continue, Detective," the man says quietly.

"Where did you go after leaving the bird cages?"

"Straight on, there is a path we like to follow."

"Did you see anyone?"

A pause, the couple look uncertain.

"Every detail is important," Fletcher says softly.

"No, we didn't see anyone," the wife says firmly.

"Was there no one walking ahead of you?"

"The park was quiet. It is November," she says pointedly.

"There was someone ahead of us," the man says.

"When?" his wife snaps. There will be discussions about this on the way home.

"I saw him before I saw her."

"What was he doing?"

"Walking away."

"What did he look like?"

"I don't know, he was too far ahead." The man looks ashamed. "I don't even know if it was a he – he was very far away."

"Did that person remind you of anyone you know?"

"Like I said, he was too far ahead."

"Did you see their clothing?"

"Was just a dark blur."

"Did you see any points of colour?"

The man shrugs helplessly. "No."

"Had you seen anyone hanging around the park? Anything you thought was suspicious or out of place?"

"It's a park," the wife says, a tad snidely.

"We don't tend to look at the people, Detective."

"The victim, did you recognise her?"

The man's eyes drop again, these are not memories he wants to think of. "No, I don't think I have seen her before."

"After you found the victim, what happened next?"

Both pairs of eyes drop, it's time for the bad memories. Fletcher waits patiently.

"I checked for a pulse. I was a volunteer with the St John's ambulance service ... I thought ... I thought maybe she was drunk ... that I could help her."

His wife softly rubs his arm supportively, he grips her hand. This, they won't talk about again.

"She was already dead." A slow pause, his mind is going

through the scene again angrily, what else does the officer want? "Then we called the police."

"Did you notice anyone else in the park then?"

"No, some more people arrived when the police arrived, but I don't remember seeing anyone before that ... it was just us and..." His voice cracks.

Fletcher ends the interview.

November 11th, 7pm

Fletcher finds himself repeatedly nodding off to sleep, always just catching himself at the last moment. It is time to go home, tomorrow he has interviews scheduled with Isobel Hilarie's mother, Madison Albrook's mother and then they are going over to examine Madison's room. There is always a small chance she had arranged to meet with the assailant, like Adelina Sasha had but unlike Adelina Sasha, maybe she had left some kind of clue behind, something more useful than the CCTV footage. Next to him, Bullface yawns, rubbing her eyes viciously. She is slowly unwrapping a bar of chocolate with numb fingers. It isn't until she finds herself tasting plastic instead of sweet sugar that she realises just how tired she is, but by then it is too late to retrieve her chocolate from the bin. She hopes Fletcher hasn't noticed. The wrapper tastes terrible.

Across the city people are watching the news in sheer disbelief. He is watching as well, his arms wrapped around his wife, comforting her. He is enjoying this, for the first time in his life, he is actually enjoying something. There are consequences of course, he had purposely let victim 22 be found publicly,

WHAT LIES IN THE DARK

knowing there would be consequences. But he wanted them to know he was out there. Thought it meant that small petty things like security would increase, already he has had to change a site because a police car was spying around the corner. But it also means that their paranoia is increasing, people are beginning to turn on each other. He grins clutching his wife tighter, indirectly he is controlling them, making them afraid of the shadows. It is a shame he had to sacrifice some of his numbers but they didn't mean that much to him, he could get more. These women mean absolutely nothing. He will have no problem getting more.

His wife shivers in his arms as the image of Madison Albrook is brought on screen.

"Are you going jogging tomorrow night?" she asks, fear lacing her voice. The very sound of her fear sends delicious shivers down his spine.

"No." He feels her slight relief. "But I am meeting Aaron for a quick drink."

He enjoys her begging him not to stay out too late. He promises to be home early but doesn't really mean it. The beer will taste so much better when he knows she is sitting, anxiously waiting for him to come home, afraid of every little noise.

November 12th, 8.08am

Fletcher sits at his desk, a cooling cup of black coffee to his right, a copy of the eyewitness statements to his left. While he was interviewing yesterday, his colleagues had gone round every vendor who operated in or near the park, every possible witness. As far as Fletcher can tell, Madison had left her house around 1.30pm going straight to a local piercing parlour. Fletcher's cheeks burn a bright red as he reads exactly what Madison had pierced. Madison left that place at 2.15pm, then she had been spotted in the supermarket. Her shopping bag had been found in the park bushes containing a bag of carrots, a jar of coffee and a bar of dark chocolate – but no purse. She had been identified only because her student card had been in her jeans pocket. Some people had seen a man waiting near the bushes, sitting on a nearby bench, some said he was a black man, some said white. He had been there out of the camera sight, for maybe an hour. He had been drinking a beverage and reading a paper, the newspaper obscuring his face from the passers-by. None of the vendors remembered selling anything to him. They had seized the litter bins within a mile radius of the park, to see if they could find what he was drinking. Unfortunately, even in winter most of the bins had been full, which meant over two hundred DNA samples taken from the two hundred and sixty-four cups and cans had to be sent to the back-logged lab. This case now had priority over every other case but it was still going to take a while.

The vendors had confirmed that this was a regular walk home for Madison, though it was not her usual time. She usually came through the park at 4.30pm with another girl. Fletcher can't help but think that if Isobel hadn't died, then maybe Madison would have gone to class as usual and would not have walked home alone.

Isobel's attack had not yet yielded any eyewitnesses, no one so much as heard a scream. The store clerk was the only one who reported seeing her and not seen anyone hanging around the store, well there had been the usual crowds but it was a cold night and no one had wanted to hang around. The clerk had a long night, another long night, then a long week, a long, overworked tired week. Everything had blurred into one. It probably meant the clerk had forgotten completely to tell them something important. They have searched the nearby bins again, searching for possible bloody clothing, Fletcher has the sinking suspicion that the assailant was taking all evidence home with him. He gags on a mouthful of cold coffee before continuing to read.

At 10.17am Fletcher is informed that Mrs Hilarie, Isobel's mother, has arrived. He does not know what to expect, half of him thinks that maybe Mrs Hilarie will be as funky as her daughter ... was. Maybe a new-age hippie sort of lady, or maybe Isobel had been rebelling against her parents and Mrs Hilarie would resemble a typical tax accountant. Fletcher takes one last look at the picture portraying the young artist with bright purple hair, smiling wildly into the camera and then goes to meet her mother.

Mrs Hilarie sits quietly at the conference table, she has neglected to brush her hair today or match her shoes. Her face is sorrowful, streaking still with tears. She fiddles with a tiger's eye ring, twisting it back and forth on her finger. She doesn't want to be here, well rarely did anyone want to be here and she seems to be filling the small room with a cloud of desolate despair.

"Good morning, Mrs Hilarie, thank you for coming in. I am Detective Sergeant Aaron Fletcher, I need to ask you a few questions about Isobel, if I may."

Mrs Hilarie nods slowly, barely looking at Fletcher.

"Is there anything I can get for you?"

She is silent for a few moments, then finally she speaks, her voice is a dull rasp. "Did she suffer?"

"I am sorry?"

"My daughter, did she suffer?"

Fletcher bows his head slightly, but still manages to meet

Mrs Hilarie's sad eyes. "No, death would have been near instantaneous."

"You would think that would be a consolation, but it isn't." She begins to cry again, half-sobbing the words, "It really isn't."

Fletcher sits in silence for a while passing Mrs Hilarie the occasional tissue.

"Mrs Hilarie, I just need to ask you a few details about your daughter, to see if there is anything she may have told you that could help catch the person who did this."

"What's the point?" she wails. "Izzie isn't going to come back."

"No, but maybe we can stop him from striking again."

She doesn't believe him and she isn't going to say so, but Fletcher can tell, just from the way her body has completely stiffened, her hands clenching and unclenching. No one, not Jack Sasha, not Robert Leona, no one seemed to believe in their ability to catch this guy. Sometimes even Fletcher doesn't believe it. But then he also knows Bullface. Bullface will never let anyone fail.

"What was Isobel like? As a person?"

"Crazy." The half laugh, half sob. "She was very open. I used to think she had ADHD because she could never stay focused on one task."

"Did she have a lot of friends?"

"Yes, she was a very friendly person." Mrs Hilarie says this almost mechanically, suddenly wanting to retreat from the sacred memories of her daughter.

"When was the last time you spoke to your daughter?"

Mrs Hilarie is silent for a few moments. Fletcher can practically see her mind trying to work it out.

"Three days ago ... she wanted to know if she could borrow some money for an art project. I didn't want to give her the money ... I know what she and her boyfriend get up to..."

Suddenly, drinking too much with a boyfriend didn't seem so bad. "But I told her I would buy the paints for her, for Christmas."

"Was she OK with that?" Fletcher asks gently.

"Izzie never had it in her, I mean, she was never mad or upset. She just accepted everything."

"Had Isobel complained of anyone following her?"

"No, Izzie would have confronted them, she is very fearless." An unwelcome memory of Izzie has flashed into her mind, a fresh supply of sobs burst forth.

There is silence for a few minutes, with Fletcher patiently passing more tissues before finally asking, "Did Isobel tend to go out alone?"

"No, no, she usually goes everywhere with her boyfriend, those two were always together ... I don't know why he let her go out alone." Her eyes are suddenly dark now that she has someone to blame. Someone she didn't think of before. Izzie's boyfriend would not be welcomed at her funeral; not that he would be sober enough to remember when it was. Mrs Hilarie's future contains a number of phone calls from him begging for forgiveness. She won't forgive him but she won't hang up either.

"Had Isobel upset anyone lately?"

"No, no ... no ... everyone liked Izzie. She was such a..." Another sob, tears staining into Mrs Hilarie's white shirt.

"You mentioned that Isobel asked you for money, do you think she may have borrowed money from someone else?" It is a long shot, a very, very long shot.

"No." Mrs Hilarie's tone is forceful, Fletcher can see that despite her current appearance, she is not someone to take advantage of. "I told Isobel never to borrow money from anyone else, she always came to me first. I know what you are thinking. Flamboyant girl always getting drunk, could be going out and doing stupid things, but Izzie isn't like that." A gasp. "Izzie wasn't like that." Mrs Hilarie passes from angry to upset within a matter of seconds, a monsoon of emotions.

"I am sorry, Mrs Hilarie, I need to ask these questions, just to make sure." Fletcher's throbbing headache is back, thumping cheerfully away at the back of his head. "Did Isobel know anyone called Madison Albrook?"

"That was the girl, on the news last night. Wasn't it?"

Fletcher nods, not wanting to give more details than necessary, the news report had made everyone aware of the connection between the girls. It was only a matter of time before Adelina Sasha and Fran Lizzie Taylor's names also rose from the dead. "My daughter had a lot of friends, there were too many for me to keep track of. I don't recognise the name though. Izzie only moved here a few months ago."

Mrs Hilarie lives about an hour's drive away from the city, enough distance for Izzie to feel some freedom without moving too far. The university had been in a great location for her, since she had loved the city so much. A little part of Mrs Hilarie is now wishing that Izzie had chosen a different university instead of following in her mother's footsteps. It would be a long empty drive home for her, with blame following closely behind her.

Fletcher views the new woman now sitting in front of him, Madison Albrook's mother, Ms Albrook. She sits in a crisp grey suit, perfectly immaculate. Her eyes are clear, solidly fixed on Fletcher's face.

"Good morning, Ms Albrook, thank you for coming in. I am Detective Sergeant Aaron Fletcher, I need to ask you a few questions about Madison, if I may."

This is beginning to become a well-rehearsed speech. To Fletcher there seems to be something very wrong about this, something is whispering in the back of his mind. It isn't because this is the fourth victim's family he has had to talk to, he is a specialist in interviewing and this is what he does all year long, interviewing victims, victims' families, eyewitnesses and suspects. What's wrong is how mechanically he is doing it, the well-rehearsed speech that requires no emotion even his sympathy is beginning to feel forced. It isn't right, nothing is right here.

"Good morning, Detective," she says softly, her voice giving a slight trace of accent. His speech may have been rehearsed but their replies are always different. Different yet still the same. Some like Mrs Hilarie are in the full stages of grief, barely keeping it together but others like Ms Albrook give the impression of a person still in control, someone who can handle the situation coolly and calmly. Fletcher doubts that the reality of the situation has hit her yet. This type is just a ticking time bomb.

"Is there anything I can get for you?" No one ever jokes here, no one asks for a million pounds or a nice car. No one asks for the impossible, no one quietly whispers that they just want their daughter back. Sometimes people ask for a drink but usually it is the autopilot response, a shake of the head or the "No, I am fine." Ms Albrook is a stern woman, breaking down and crying in front of a police officer would be an intolerable weakness. Jokes are a no-go area so that just leaves the quiet, "No, thank you, Detective."

"Ms Albrook, I just need to ask you a few details about your daughter, to see if there is anything she may have told you that could help catch the person who did this." He speaks softly, taking care not to mix up the names – to accidentally say Isobel instead of Madison. Ms Albrook nods quickly, just wanting to get on with it.

"What was Madison like? As a person?"

"She was..." Ms Albrook hadn't always noticed Madison as

a person. "...quiet, she liked to study. She always had her nose in a book."

"Did she have a lot of friends?"

"She never really mentioned any friends."

"Did she have a boyfriend?"

"No."

"When was the last time you spoke to your daughter?"

A pause, Madison had not come home for the summer as she had a summer job somewhere, Ms Albrook hadn't asked where it was and Madison hadn't said. The sudden realisation hits Ms Albrook that it was November, meaning the last time she had actually seen her daughter was ... Christmas last year, eleven months ago. Even then at Christmas Madison had spent a lot of time in her room, she had coursework to do and Ms Albrook just let her get on with it. When was the last time Madison had phoned? A sudden panic fills Ms Albrook, she does not want to be seen as a bad mother.

"Last weekend, I think or maybe the weekend before that," she lies uneasily.

"Had Madison seemed emotional? Was she happy? Upset?"

"No, she seemed ... fine, just her normal self really."

Fletcher notices that her carefully polished fingernails have recently been viciously bitten down and her hands are now shaking slightly. Sometimes trembling or shaking hands are taken as signs of guilt or an indicator that the speaker is lying whereas calm steady hands are taken as a sign that the speaker is calm, perhaps honest or a well-practised sociopathic liar. Fletcher doesn't think Ms Albrook is lying to him but maybe she is feeling guilty about something.

"Had Madison complained of anyone following her?"

"No, I don't think she did, people didn't tend to notice Madison in that way."

"Did Madison tend to go out alone?"

"No, Madison was a very responsible girl."

Ah, Fletcher thinks quietly to himself, sometimes parents are the last ones to know, but then most other people have been saying similar things about Madison Albrook. The quiet, responsible girl that no one really noticed, the complete opposite of Isobel Hilarie.

"Had Madison upset anyone lately?"

"No, Madison wasn't the type..."

"Did Madison know anyone called Isobel Hilarie?"

"No." Ms Albrook doesn't even recognise the name.

"Did Madison know anyone called Fran Lizzie Taylor?"

"No." She doesn't recognised that name either. A second wave of panic hits Ms Albrook, were these her daughter's friends? Should she recognise the names?

"My daughter and I aren't very close," she mumbles in a way of apology, eyes suddenly downcast. Fletcher isn't quite sure who she is apologising to.

One of the last people to speak to Madison Albrook sits, polluting the small conference room. Fletcher is tempted to open the door, strongly tempted, privacy and confidentiality be damned. The source of the smell sits in the chair opposite, a dowdy older lady, wearing a shabby raincoat in stained pink. It is the first time Mrs Chalmers has left her small apartment in years. For the sake of the nice-ish girl who had lived upstairs, Mrs Chalmers is forsaking her afternoon soaps, with a small amount of regret. If only she had a son talented enough to be able to programme a VCR.

Fletcher coughs slightly the distinctive musky perfume is irritating his senses, burning his throat and the unmasked clear smell of body odour is slamming itself into his nose, Fletcher is trying unsuccessfully to breathe through his ears.

"Good afternoon, Mrs Chalmers, I am Detective Sergeant Aaron Fletcher. Thank you for coming in. I would like to ask you a few questions about Madison Albrook, if I may?"

Mrs Chalmers has never been inside a police station before. After a lifetime of watching soaps and dramas she was expecting something a little more … glamorous. Instead she has been ushered into a dark dingy room, no one has so much as shown her a crime scene photo. She is very, very disappointed.

"Now, Madison Albrook was your neighbour?" he asks.

"Yes, she lived upstairs from me."

"How well did you know her?"

"She was a very quiet girl, I kept asking her to join Augustus and me for dinner, she always refused. She was such a shy girl."

"What sort of routine did Madison have?"

"Well … she usually went to her classes every day, she was a student, you know, some kind of ology, I always told her she should concentrate on her looks not her books, but you know what kids are like these days, just full of big ideas. Augustus was never like that … Augustus is my son, I always thought they would make a good couple. She was just too shy to talk to him. Augustus is an artist, you know."

Fletcher doesn't know. What he does know is that Madison did not have classes every day, her schedule showed that she was in class three days a week, and worked only one day a week. The chance that Madison had a secret in her life was high, though maybe it wasn't that secret; just no one had bothered to ask.

"How had Madison seemed emotionally recently? Did she seem upset or happy to you?"

Mrs Chalmers frowns, the last memory of Madison telling her almost gleefully where she was going floats in her mind. Nice girls did not do things like that. Mrs Chalmers suspects that maybe Madison had been joking.

"She seemed ... her usual self really, she was just quiet." She speaks sullenly, she is missing her afternoon soaps for this? "I told her to be careful out on the streets, that there was a monster out there. She should have listened to me or taken Augustus with her. He's my son, you know, Augustus, he's an artist."

Fletcher makes a mental note to have Augustus investigated, either Mrs Chalmers is hinting at something or she is being incredibly annoying.

"Did Madison receive many visitors in her flat?"

"She used to have a flatmate, a really loud noisy girl. I had to complain to the landlord about her. I told Madison she was far too much of a nice girl to put up with someone like that."

"Do you remember the flatmate's name?" No one else had mentioned a flatmate.

"It was something really Zsah ... Zsaha ... Zahaia ... something like that." Mrs Chalmers wrinkles her over-powdered nose in distaste.

Fletcher thoughtfully writes the names down. "Had Madison complained of anyone following her recently?"

"No, certainly not. We live in a good area," she says angrily. We are not the common people, her tone implies.

Fletcher fights to keep his face impassive, fighting back against the smell and distaste. "Have you seen anyone suspicious around the flats recently?" He asks the question slowly, knowing the question will annoy Mrs Chalmers even more.

She gives him another angry look, not quite managing to be threatening. "What do you mean by that, young man?"

"Have you seen anyone in your area who isn't usually there? Someone who doesn't belong there, looks out of place."

"Certainly not, I would have called the police if I had."

Fletcher slowly thanks her for her help, gives the standard

"please feel free to contact me if you remember any more details" then ushers her out of the door.

Mrs Chalmers's overpowering scent follows him as he grabs a quick lunch in the police canteen. He had been too tired to eat breakfast this morning and his stomach is now angrily protesting. He had been too tired for dinner last night too. Claire hadn't saved him any leftovers and was already asleep when he got home, even in sleep she was giving him the cold shoulder. Just because he said he was going to grab a quick drink with the lads tonight. But, oh no, he isn't even allowed that anymore, Claire just doesn't understand how badly he needs a break.

The police canteen is full of officers and admin clerks. Fletcher feels them stare at him accusingly, as if to ask, what are you doing here? You should be working! There will be time for food when this monster is caught. Why haven't you caught this guy yet? He grabs a ham sandwich and a coffee before retreating to sit alone in the corner. No one joins him. The food tastes like dry sawdust in his mouth and is hard to swallow.

CHAPTER EIGHT

This afternoon's main feature is a mandatory meeting for everyone working with Fletcher and Bullrush. Mostly it is a recap of the information given in the previous meeting, the personal details of the victims, the methods of murder, explanations and apologies for not already catching this guy. Bullface knows and Fletcher suspects, that other officers have already approached the Chief Constable asking for command of the case. Chief James Morkam has so far refused but Bullface knows it is only a matter of time. So far, there isn't a single action of hers that could be criticised, she hasn't missed any opportunities, unlike Fletcher, although Fletcher technically cannot be blamed for missing the blood trail. They are still the most experienced and senior officers. Bullface also knows that several other officers are investigating the case on the sly, particularly the ones who had been close to Robert Leona, but they also keep punching into dead ends. She almost welcomes their second pair of eyes but watches them closely. No one is going to make her the station's scapegoat.

They discuss possible ways of capture – 4.5 million people's DNA samples are accessible on their database but there are at least 53 million other people in the country. Their assailant is one person or maybe two people out of those 53 million people. None of the DNA samples so far collected matches anyone in the database, maybe the samples collected following Isobel Hilarie's and Madison Albrook's deaths would help narrow down the possibilities – they just need a match. If only they could force all males in the city to submit a DNA sample. Not only would that be hugely expensive and time-consuming but also a human rights infringement. But it would help catch the bastard ... and probably solve sixty per cent of their other open cases too. In Bullface's dream world, the whole world is a DNA database and they execute most criminals – consequences be damned. In Fletcher's dream world, no crimes would be committed in the first place, no one has the ability or imagination to commit crimes, they would never dream of doing something so shocking. In Fletcher's dream world, he would be a fisherman not a police officer.

"The fact that he operates during the day and night would suggest he is either unemployed or works odd hours, possibly a job which requires him to work shifts. Statements given by Adelina Sasha's friends suggest she met her attacker whilst she was out jogging. This, combined with the fact that his dump sites appear to be well planned, suggests he spends a lot of time outside on the streets scoping out new targets. I wonder if it would be beneficial to have female and male officers also on the street, undercover."

One officer, one that Bullface particularly does not like, speaks smugly. "The method of kill typically has been a slit throat, in some cases evidence suggests that the victims had no prior warning, no chance to defend themselves. If we put female officers undercover on the street then we are just practically giving the assailant more victims."

"We could increase the number of undercover male police officers on the streets."

"Who could we use? Most of our undercover officers are already on other assignments and cannot be pulled."

"We could use regular officers."

"The problem with regular officers is that they are easy to spot, even undercover. You can take the uniform off but they are still police officers," Bullface argues.

"The assailant may avoid areas where he can see other males on the street. So far he has attacked in empty areas."

Bullface looks at the three bickering officers with disappointment, this is their finest? Though to their credit most of them are actually good cops, until they have to work with each other.

"I don't think many of our officers, male or female will be willing to work undercover after what happened to Shannon," she says quietly. "If we put an undercover officer out there, then they would be working without a weapon, no chance of even being able to defend themselves should a situation arise. Even the citizens are beginning to arm themselves."

"We need to be seen doing something," the Chief says.

"We could ask for volunteers to go undercover, I know many of the officers want to help, if we get them to areas where we can monitor them easily on the CCTV circuit, increase patrols in areas most likely to be targeted."

"But we are risking their lives."

"We are risking the lives of innocents!"

"No matter what we do, the killer is going to keep attacking until he has been caught." It is always the quietest voices that say things that no one wants to hear.

"We should consider working with the media."

"Working with the media would increase the paranoia!"

"We can use the media to control the paranoia," Bullface

says thoughtfully. "Also to step up the appeals for information. Someone out there has had to have noticed this man by now. We can give a basic description to the media." A very basic description.

"With the amount of news vans trawling the areas, they will probably catch the assailant before we do," the first officer glumly mutters.

Fletcher finally makes a contribution to the conversation. "We weren't able to stop Shannon Leona's death or Madison Albrook's from making the news. The deaths were too public. It's only a matter of time before people start screaming serial killer. We need to keep the media under control, use them to soothe the public. There has already been one death because the public are afraid."

The Chief nods.

"There has been a death?"

"Man tried to sneak into his house drunk, his wife panicked and hit him with a golf club. He died a few hours ago."

"As you said already, Bull... rush, some members of the public are beginning to openly arm themselves. We need to control this before anyone else gets hurt."

"Is it ethical to disarm the public?"

"Not everyone is carrying a weapon to protect themselves."

"A media appeal for information seems to be the best suggestion, we need to warn the public that they will be arrested for carrying weapons in public. Stress that females should not be walking anywhere alone." The Chief pauses. "We will ask for officers to volunteer to go undercover and increase the patrols. I will cancel all holiday leave and ask for an increase in the budget for overtime. Are there any other suggestions?"

"We could set up a stall in the city centre to hand out rape alarms and suggest other ways of protection," Bullface says. One of the officers nods in support.

"We are focusing all our energy on catching the killer, should we not also continue the search for the other victims?" Sometimes Fletcher just has to say something stupid. Some of the other officers look at him in clear distaste.

"We could use only male volunteers this time," Bullface says quickly.

"I don't think we have enough officers, budget or time to continue the search," the Chief counteracts before anyone else can speak.

Fletcher opens his mouth as if to argue but then closes it quickly when he sees Bullface glaring at him.

"If we have an indication that there are other bodies out there, we will look for them, after the killer has been caught." After all, the dead always stay dead.

He is out shopping. There are one or two items his wife has timidly asked him to pick up and since he is such a good husband, well how can he say no? He likes being out on the streets anyway. He has always felt freer this way. He smiles to himself, knowing the reason he is out here instead of with his wife is because she is too afraid to leave the house on her own. In fact, there aren't any women out alone on the streets right now. He has made everyone afraid. He has just passed a couple now, she is wearing a yellow jumper, black skirt and has the left arm of her boyfriend protectively around her shoulders. The boyfriend is wearing jeans, a light shirt and is carrying a cricket bat in his right hand. The look on this boyfriend's face is unmistakable – *Leave my girl alone.* It is not the first couple he has passed who are carrying weapons. It is a delicious feeling, knowing they are all afraid of him. Maybe he should play with one of these couples, bait them into a frenzy. Just whisper in one's ear, "*That guy over there, yes, that guy, I seen him watching your girl, mate, better watch out.*" Just to set a spark or two flying, but then that would mean they saw him, face to face. They might remember ... but it could be fun. He needs some fun right now, he knows that two deaths in one day means even more security increases, more cops on the street, the bait staying safely at home. Even he, the cops' best friend, would be regarded with suspicion if he is spotted on the streets alone too many times. It will start to fade soon, in a few weeks, they will calm down. Then it will be time again.

He walks into the local hardware store, he has promised his wife that he will buy and install a second lock on their front door. So she can sleep at night. He notices with an increasing amount of glee that the store has odd gaps on the shelves, they have sold out of padlocks, combination locks and dead bolts. He smiles, they are afraid on the streets, in their own houses, they are afraid of their own shadows. The fun is definitely beginning now.

The university announces that it will be closed for the entire week out of respect for Madison Albrook and Isobel Hilarie. A large number of the female students have decided to leave the city, return home until the killer has been caught. Some of these students will never come back. Friends of Isobel Hilarie petition the Dean for permission to paint a mural for the two students. This is denied – the Dean has seen their art work before. A commemoration plaque is set up along with a memorial tree. Out of protest or maybe just in grief the friends and other students tie black ribbons on the tree branches. The university also holds a large memorial service for the two students, which receives a small amount of media coverage. Students are encouraged to read testimonies, some speak of Sir Izz the Mad, the fearless art student and her antics, shocking several attendees. One girl stands holding a sign that says, *Save a dragon, kill a princess,* which Isobel had previously illustrated with images of dragons and fierce princesses. A few people even speak about Madison Albrook, her lecturer speaks of a quiet girl that people didn't notice as much as they should have done, but a girl the world is going to miss.

The memorial services held by the university precedes the funerals by three days. The Dean sends shock and anger cascading through the student body when he announces a strict curfew on the students. He states that campus security will be increased. That everyone on campus must now wear an ID badge, anyone without a badge will be escorted off campus. The students are outraged, protesting that this is an infringement of their human rights, arguing that the university has no right, pointing out that the murders have all taken place off campus. The students are caught protesting on a local TV channel and heavily criticised. The curfew is eventually revoked.

He watches the students on the news with interest. The film team has done a good job of catching the rowdiest of protesters, contrasting them sharply with the monstrous images of Madison Albrook's death. The student protests also mean that the seriousness of the two females' deaths is downplayed. He is intrigued. Perhaps he should teach them all a lesson and commit the next murder on campus, but then he doesn't know the campus too well, knows there will be higher security risks. It doesn't seem worth it. He is also hopeful that the reaction of the students is an indication of what the reaction of the public will be should a city-wide curfew be imposed: that any official attempt to protect the people will be seen as "infringement of their human rights" and largely ignored.

The local news is dominated by footage of the protesting students and police appeals for information, asking if anyone can give any information on a man around six feet tall, who was wearing dark clothes, last seen around the park on November 11th.

This is something Elizabeth Mitchell notes grimly.

The Chief Constable also appears regularly on television, warning the citizens of the city not to carry weapons in the street.

"*It is dangerous and illegal, anyone caught carrying weapons in public will be arrested and prosecuted. I understand that many of you are afraid right now but this is not the answer. Anyone who feels unsafe or threatened should call the police immediately on the hotline number. I would like to remind all females not to walk alone, especially at night. There are some special seminars being held.*" He lists the times, locations and dates slowly. "*These seminars will include instructions on how to protect yourself and your family. I would like to stress again that no one, no one should be carrying weapons on the streets. This will not be tolerated.*"

Madison Albrook's funeral is held the day before Isobel's. Her mother decides to bury her in the city, rather than bring her home. Madison had just never belonged at home. Her father chooses not to attend. For once, Madison's mother doesn't complain, it doesn't feel right to have him there. It doesn't feel right that she herself attends. She didn't know the girl, but everyone seems to be grieving for a remarkable girl while she is there out of ... obligation? Duty? Demand? Why is she here? Did Madison actually mean something to her? It is with a stony face she acknowledges the other mourners, refusing to allow herself to be pulled into hugs, refusing to even cry. No one knows her here, they call her Mrs Albrook instead of Ms. They remind her of what and who she has lost over the years without knowing the whys. They don't have the right to hug her, she ignores them all, her eyes stay firmly fixed on the wooden coffin that contains her only daughter.

"Dearly beloved..."

She just doesn't know what to feel. During the service, something breaks as she slowly stands up, without saying anything or looking at anyone and hurries away. Ignoring her family's calls, rushing past Madison's friends and an astonished Jennifer Taylor. She leaves the funeral before her daughter is even lowered into the ground. One lone camera snaps her behaviour, catching the normally tall, proud Ms Albrook just as she is leaving, catching the astonished, angry bereaved faces calling after her but not catching the single tear that is sliding down Ms Albrook's face.

Isobel Hilarie's funeral is a little different. It would have been disappointing to Isobel. Isobel would have been startled maybe even amused to see some of her friends with a fresh haircuts, some even wearing suits and even sober. She would have been sad to know Frank didn't make it. She would have been happy to see her father comforting her mother, despite the angry looks from her stepmother. Isobel wouldn't know the mousy woman who approached her mother at the end of the service. Out of sight from the other mourners Jennifer Taylor and Mrs Hilarie murmur, close to the grave of Fran Lizzie Taylor before a firm NO! is said and one turns away with anger and tears in her eyes.

Three days after Madison's funeral Ms Albrook is accosted on the stairs by an extremely smelly but chatty woman. In the last three days Ms Albrook hasn't talked to anyone, hasn't answered her phone. In her mind, she has a plan, she is going to empty Madison's flat, the rent will be running out soon and Ms Albrook doesn't want to pay another month's worth, not when no one will be using it. She has charity bags ready, then this will be over and then she is going to go home, go back to work and just ... forget. This seems the most practical of solutions, this is what is going through her head as the smelly woman prattles on and on about how sorry she is for her loss. Ms Albrook has heard that a lot recently. I am sorry for your loss, it doesn't really feel like she has lost something. Ms Albrook doesn't really feel anything. Mrs Chalmers babbles about her son, Augustus, how he is going to make a mural for Madison, something to honour her memory. Ms Albrook barely hears any of this. In her mind she is just concentrating on doing this and getting home. Quietly she says goodbye to Mrs Chalmers and rudely walks off. Mrs Chalmers glares after her for a brief moment then scurries back into her flat, to complain to Augustus.

Madison had been renting a flat above Mrs Chalmers, a two-bedroomed flat that currently has one bedroom empty. Well two empty bedrooms now. Madison's previous flatmate had moved out two months before and Madison had been looking for a replacement. Ms Albrook would never know that Madison was planning to have her girlfriend move in. Madison's previous flatmate would not be found by the police. The girlfriend would never admit anything to anyone.

Ms Albrook calmly unlocks the door, she has been here before, when Madison first moved in, supervising the move. Now the flat looks different, the police have left behind only a slight impression of violation. In their search, they have left drawers open, other things just slightly out of place. Despite this, it looks different because it has touches of Madison in it. It is Madison's clothes that cover the floor. It is Madison's art prints on the walls. Ms Albrook casts her eye over the Asian, Mexican and spicy food cook books that fill Madison's bookshelves, fitting neatly with Madison's criminology text books and romance novels. She didn't know her daughter liked to cook, it wasn't really done in their house. She didn't know her daughter had seriously considered switching from criminology to food technology or dropping out altogether to train as a chef.

The walls have been painted a pretty yellow colour, giving the room a warm welcoming vibe that Ms Albrook had never known. Looking around the abandoned room, she realises that there was a lot she had never known and now never will.

Brandi is realising just how much she hates her life. Her mother is a consistent nagging harpy, perching firmly on her shoulder. The attacks mean that her mother is calling every single day now, "*Just to make sure you are OK.*" Any excuse to jabber on about her sister's new jewellery and how Brandi should go around to meet the new man. "*He does have a brother darling, recently divorced.*" Brandi has no desire to meet her sister's new toy or his brother. She does not want to see her brand-new house or the new jewellery that is 14 carat gold. "*Real diamonds, darling,*" her mother always has to says breathlessly. So what?

Brandi hates her mother, hates hates hates her. Hates her sister, stupid bitch, just because she got the good hair, the good face. No one tells her sister that her nose is too big, her sister never gets as much as a pimple. Stupid fucking bitch.

How sorry would they be if she got attacked? Would that finally make her the honoured daughter? Not even her mother would speak ill of the dead. She could be the favoured daughter then ... and what if she caught this guy? Lured him and caught him? Suck on your diamonds then, sister, I caught the bad guy. I am the hero ... Brandi suddenly smiles. The male sitting opposite her on the bus looks away quickly, there is something about that smile that almost seems ... predatory.

A seventy-two-year-old woman is not usually a scary predator – usually. Unknown to Brandi Parr, her predatory smile is being copied by Elizabeth Mitchell, only Elizabeth's smile is even creepier as her pearly white false teeth glimmer from behind her purple drapes. He has gone. She has waited forty minutes to make sure he isn't coming back. He has definitely gone. Her arthritic hands shake with excitement as she grips Old Arnie's key. One quick glance tells her the street is empty. Her neighbour to the left is visiting her grandchildren for two weeks and the house to the right has been empty for several months. No one will see, no one will know. She walks quickly out of her front door, straight past her beautiful garden and across the road into his not so beautiful yard where he has let the rubbish bags pile and fester. Elizabeth feels certain that one of those bags will contain ... no, she will "borrow" the bags later, she can go through those in her own house. Slowly she clicks Old Arnie's key in the door and pushes it open. A smell immediately drafts through to her wrinkled nose. A rancid foul odour, as she closes the door behind her softly Elizabeth sees just what is causing that odour.

CHAPTER NINE

Number 32 has not yet rotted. He had killed her back in October but the onset of cold weather means that she is slow to decompose. How annoying. Perhaps he will stick her with the others. He can't leave her where she is for much longer. They might start looking again and she is a little too obvious. In life as in death, she has always been a little too obvious. No one has missed her yet, that was a good start. No one really misses people like her, do they? He didn't even want her. He deserved better than her, but he needed her, needed that release. Maybe he should let her be discovered. Maybe little Roxanne needs her moment in the spotlight. That moment she had craved her entire life. Ha ha.

Oh what to do, what to do? He could put her with the others, she would rot eventually, wouldn't she? The cold temperatures won't preserve her forever. Could stick her with the other numbers, it is getting crowded though. He can barely move in there now, without stepping into something icky. Maybe he should get rid of them all. One big massive bonfire. Let the city choke on the flames of its dead. Maybe he should give them all to his good buddy Aaron, he might appreciate the early Christmas present. Then Aaron could take care of them all. He definitely doesn't want them anymore. He has other things to remember them by and now they are just in the way. Keeping them could be dangerous, especially if they start to figure things out, if they actually realise what's going on. Maybe he could play them, tell the world how to find them. Set up a few "accidents" for the search crews and scare them all even more. If he does it right then maybe he could even make them turn on each other. Keep on increasing that fear. But then that would make it harder to hunt. He likes challenges but that's how people get caught, isn't it? Going too fast taking too many risks, taking stupid chances. People like Aaron aren't that stupid; they will start to discover things. Maybe they already knew one or two things. If he gives the other girls to the city, they might find something, that little hint, then he will have to find a new city, new places to hunt. He likes hunting here, it is his home. No, for now they can stay where they are, it isn't like anyone is going to find them any time soon is it? Maybe he should think of ways to make them a little less obvious, do a little more digging before the ground freezes.

Still, what to do with Roxanne? Little Miss Number 32. He could just send her to Aaron, one little gift. That would be fun, wouldn't it? But then how to give Roxanne to Aaron ... it isn't like he could just leave her on Aaron's doorstep, could he? He probably won't appreciate her either. She would be wasted on Aaron and he had gone to so much trouble too.

He needs to hunt again soon. He is impatient, the cold nights and his wife mean that jogging is out of the question. Maybe he needs to cool down a little anyway, he doesn't want to be caught, he is having too much fun. If he goes out too much without a good reason, his wife might get suspicious, maybe he will have to deal with her. But then how to do it? He would need a good alibi. If she went missing he would be an immediate suspect. They would notice if she went missing too. Even if she wasn't found they would still suspect him. Investigate him! It is too close a link. Right now no one suspects him and he can continue. But he does so badly want to get rid of her; she is annoying him. At first her fear amused him, but now she is irritating, a constant wet blanket. There has to be an easy way to get rid of her. She is nosey, maybe he could exploit that? Set up a beautifully tragic accident for her. Thinking of a non-suspicious way to get rid of her is something that will keep him occupied for a while, something to think about.

She can't be allowed to live for much longer, oh no. Christmas is coming, a lot of accidents happen around Christmas, don't they? Cars accidentally slide off roads, Christmas lights have been known to explode, and whole houses can just catch fire.

Elizabeth Mitchell stands in his front room, too scared to move her feet. All over the floor are scattered takeaway boxes, growing mould and releasing rancid odour into the air. Piles of dirty plates are stacked. A drum kit stands proudly, covered in dust. In front of her is a dirty grey-stained sofa. Little splats of curry dot the floor, weird little splats of ... something else cover the walls. She stands, too disgusted to move, scared to move her feet in case she stands in something. Part of her screams to get out, to let the police handle this. But they can't do anything can they? Not unless they have some sort of proof, and she owes it to those girls to find proof. It has to be him she just needs to prove it. He always went out whenever there was a murder. He is six foot. He is always wearing black. She just needs some proof it's him, something. She edges one foot forward slowly. Where is best to start? She has an hour or two before he will come screeching back. Where do serial killers keep their evidence? A wild giggle escapes her throat. The bedroom maybe? Or the bottom of the garden? Old Arnie did have a dilapidated garden shed. She creeps into the kitchen and stops again.

Elizabeth hears the noise first. The constant drip, drip, drip, combined with the buzz of a refrigerator. Drip, drip, drip. Her eyes begin to adjust to the gloom. The sink is filled with rotting plates. Another overpowering smell hits as she creeps closer to look through the dirty window and sees that the plates in the sink are covered in a thick layer of green mould, she thinks she can see things … wriggling. The smell is overwhelming, the deaths of a thousand takeaways waft through. Drip, drip, drip. She turns, that sound is definitely not coming from the rusty taps. She imagines blood dripping, almost hopes it is, as that means she can leave and call the police. She moves closer to the sound, drip, drip, drip. A cold wet dot falls down on her cheek.

"Oh get off your high mountain, Aaron," Claire shrieks in a high-pitched fury. Fletcher's parents when they were naming him, did not know that Aaron meant High Mountain. Unfortunately Claire does. Fletcher sometimes wishes that Claire meant daughter of the dog or lopsided cow.

Fletcher takes a deep breath and tries to assure himself that they are both adults, they can talk this through calmly and rationally. "I just wish you would consider this."

"I said no. I am not going."

"You would be safer, it will only be for a little while."

"A little while? Do you have any idea what a little while would do to my career? Do you?"

"You could still commute in."

"No, Aaron."

"Claire."

"Don't you 'Claire' me. I am not going to stay with my

mother." A cup, still half full of coffee twists dangerously in Claire's hands. Her brown eyes flush with anger.

"It's for your own safety. There is a killer out there."

"I don't care. I am not going."

"Claire, please just consider this. Be reasonable."

"You be reasonable. For all you know this guy could have left the city by now."

"He hasn't."

"You don't know that." The cup is twisting faster, small drips of coffee add to the already stained floor.

"I just want you to be safe."

"That's not what this is about, is it?"

"Yes, it is."

"No, you don't want me around anymore, that's what you are trying to say."

"No, Claire."

Why on earth would she think that?

"Yes it is, this is why you have been working overtime, isn't it? You don't want me to be around anymore."

"That's not true." Dear lord, where has this come from?

"Don't lie to me."

"I just want you to be safe."

"Are you having an affair?"

"What? No."

"Liar."

"Claire, you know that's not true."

Is she trying to manipulate him? Overexaggerate the situation so he would give in to her? Or did she genuinely think that this is what it is about? Sometimes Claire confuses him more than anything.

There is a fierce stony silence. Fletcher decides it is just best to compromise now, he is beginning to wish he hadn't said anything.

"Look, I just want you to be safe, if you don't want to go then fine stay here. I am just trying to protect you, that's all."

"Oh sure, that's what you want, isn't it? For me to stay here like a good little housewife."

He isn't going to win this one, no matter what he says. "Claire."

"Fuck you, Aaron." The cup is flung in his general direction, splattering coffee over the cream walls as Claire triumphantly storms out the house. Fletcher sits among the shards, trying to figure out just where he has gone wrong.

Elizabeth Mitchell's heart trembles as the drops continue to slither down her face. Her eyes see a dark patch slowly growing on the ceiling, dripping down into the sink. Elizabeth's skin crawls, the whole house seems to be oozing suffocating dirt. How could someone live like this? She moves across the kitchen floor, her feet sticking with each step, not daring to think about what she is stepping in. Peering out the dirty windows she sees the neglected back garden. Old Arnie's prized shed is barely visible through the thick grass. No one had been out in that garden for a long time. No, that isn't his lair. It has to be somewhere in here. Somewhere in the house is evidence that he killed those girls.

Elizabeth had first become suspicious after Fran Lizzie's death. He had come home that night roaring drunk, shouting that it wasn't his fault over and over again. She had thought little of it at the time; such antics were not unusual for him. Then she had seen that picture of the poor girl. There had been something not quite right about that young man, she had seen it since the day he moved in. Something not quite right at all. She started watching him more closely then. Back in March, he had been quiet, no more drunken nights ... for a while anyway. Just sitting in the front room, smoking cigarette after cigarette. She has monitored him for months, carefully recording his every coming and going, waiting for him to slip up. Even waiting with the video camera, just waiting for him to lose it again. Something so she could prove her suspicions to the police. He must have known that she was watching as he started being careful. But she knew she would get him eventually, he would pay for what he had done. She had almost given up when he started drinking again back in July. Literally stumbling home to collapse on the grass, singing satanic songs to the sky.

Then from 20th August to 1st September he did not come home at all. She had first thought he was on some kind of holiday until she heard about what happened to those three women. It had to have been him, he must have been hiding somewhere, scared that the police were coming by. Had to have been him. His drinking had got worse when he came home in September. Elizabeth observed that he was leaving for the shops every single day for more cigarettes and beer. He was a man falling apart she had decided, couldn't live with himself after what he had done. But she wasn't going to let him get away with it, oh no. She has been waiting for the right time to come in and snoop. The proof is somewhere in this house and she is going to get it. That just leaves upstairs. She isn't so good with stairs anymore. Each step will bring a jab of pain to her ankles. She needs take stairs very slowly at home – she doesn't know if she will have that much time. Sudden panic overwhelms her, no one knows she is in here. She hadn't even told her husband. He had already denounced her suspicions as mad, if he knew she had come in here alone ... should she go upstairs? If he comes home suddenly, she won't be able to get downstairs. She will be trapped in the house. He would notice the front door unlocked ... her mind starts screaming that she should get out of here, get out now. She is crazy to be here, in the house belonging to a man she suspects is a serial killer. No, no she can do this. He won't be home for a while, she is sure of that. It could be days until he comes back, she is being stupid for no reason. She has to do this! Slowly she starts to creak towards the stairs.

Bullface is spending her day off alone. She has told her husband she is working. Not that he really cares where she is. None of them care, she had been happier with her first husband but he can't stand the sight of her anymore. That's why she ended up marrying Mr Bullrush, her second husband. If she hadn't married him she wouldn't have gained that stupid nickname. No one would call her Bullface if she was still called Mrs Tanner, Mrs Victoria Tanner, mother of Pippa Tanner. Instead of Victoria Bullrush, mother to two large hairy bastards – Cain and Abel reincarnated. Bullface is spending her day off alone, with a near-empty bottle of brandy. A second bottle is waiting faithfully by her side. She just can't be bothered to do anything else today. So what if she needs to buy Christmas presents for her boys, it isn't like they are four anymore. Christmas is just an excuse to them now, an excuse to extort more money out of her. In another year or two they might move out, hopefully, then maybe she will ask for a divorce or maybe they should stop pretending now. Oh fucking Christmas! Pippa would be twenty-two now. Just like Fran Lizzie Taylor.

How could she celebrate Christmas? There is another fucking one of them on the loose. No matter how hard she works, they keep coming back. Keep coming back for more and more lives. No matter what she does they come back. She is supposed to keep them off the streets. She isn't doing her job properly if they keep coming back. She is trying so hard to stop them, working as long as she can, as hard as she can but it means nothing, he is still out there. It's been months now and he is still out there. Just waiting, he is going to kill someone else. He is going to kill someone else and it will be her fault. She gulps back another glassful of the light amber liquid, amber like Pippa's hair. Quietly, alone in the empty house, Bullface begins to cry.

Elizabeth Mitchell stares up. The stairs are littered with empty whiskey bottles; the smell of alcohol is overwhelming. One little flame, her mind suddenly thinks, one little flame. That's all it would take, just one little tiny flame. No, that isn't right. None of this is right. Maybe, maybe, he knows she has been watching him, maybe he has booby trapped the stairs. Maybe he is expecting her. He is smart, smart enough to elude the police for this long. Maybe he has been smart enough to booby trap his house. Maybe he is just waiting outside, smiling to himself. He doesn't like her, she knows that much. He doesn't really like anyone. Killing her would mean nothing to him. All it would take is one little match, one little flame. No, she is sure he has gone. He wouldn't have set a trap, he doesn't know she has a key. No, it is safe. She takes a deep soothing breath, inhaling more of the acidic whiskey aroma, trying to calm herself. She needs to do this, needs to prove to her husband and to herself that she isn't crazy. No, she isn't crazy. It is him killing those girls, and she knows it. Has to be him and he has to be stopped.

If the house burns down, no one would know that she is in here. They might not ever find her. All the evidence would be gone too, maybe he has planned this. Maybe it isn't her he is planning to kill. Her mind races with possibilities. He hates cops, doesn't he? He killed that special constable. Maybe he has called the police already, planning to send a group of them down in a funeral pyre of flames. No, no, she can't let that happen. She is over-thinking this, overestimating him. She just wants to get out of here but can't. It is as if the upper floor is beckoning to her, flashing his secrets at her. The answers are upstairs. She needs to go upstairs. Nothing will happen. Defiantly she begins to climb the steps, slowly and painfully. Her hands shaking, just waiting for the one little flame.

The café is quiet. There is a faint buzz in the background as one of the waiters tries unsuccessfully to flirt with a lone waitress. But she is far too old to be flirted with. She used to like this restaurant. Used to come in here all the time to meet her daughter. The café has been designed with a Mexican theme. The walls are a warming reddish orange and cactuses are dotted in strange places. Her daughter the traveller said that they served the best coffee she had ever tasted. The coffee that tastes so bitter now. Jennifer tries to disguise the lone tear now falling down her face, quickly with the cactus-shaped napkins. When she looks up again she sees two men sadly staring down at her. She clears her throat softly, motioning for them to take a seat.

"Thank you for joining me," Jennifer Taylor says quietly, still stabbing at the traitorous tears.

The bathroom makes the rest of the house look like a palace. Elizabeth Mitchell can definitely see things moving in here. Little black dots amidst the shallow dirty pools of pungent water and the abandoned stained towels. Bigger dots than what she thought she saw in the kitchen. A faded white sink is miserably overflowing, spilling more dirty water over the sides and through the kitchen ceiling. Nothing will make Elizabeth venture any further into this bathroom. Her skin crawls. No, she doesn't need to look in this room and she won't look in this room. That just leaves two other rooms. She continues along the filthy hallway, one room has the door wide open, letting rays of light into the otherwise gloomy hallway. Old Arnie would have been depressed to see how his house has been abused, depressed and disgusted. Her ears imagine they can hear skittering noises or scratching, did he have a girl here? She pushes open his bedroom door and gasps.

CHAPTER TEN

The heating has never worked quite right in Kain's house. As Kain sits at the computer, he can feel the cold spreading to fingers and toes. Doesn't matter that the only thing that is actually exuding heat is the lit cigarette. Kain has another five hundred cigarettes, packed neatly alongside sixteen jars of instant coffee. He will be safe here for a little while longer. It will be safe soon, it will be safe soon, it will be safe soon.

Bullface's mobile shrills through her drunken glaze, breaking through the thick cloud of alcohol-induced depression. Her first thought is just to ignore it. This is her day off, why are they contacting her on her day off? Can't she just have one day away from them? It isn't like she is able to help them anyway, she is just useless. But there are several things that would make them call her on her day off. First, there has been an accident involving her family. Second, there is someone requesting to speak to her. Third, there has been another murder, specifically another murder involving a victim with a number carved into their hand. The phone continues to ring impatiently. With shaky hands she finally presses answer. A voice buzzes through the line, sobering Bullface with every tone. Finally she smiles.

"We are just visiting the grandparents at the moment, I am three hours away but I will leave now," she lies. Three hours should be long enough to sober up, she decides as she heads for the shower. Enough time to get rid of the evidence.

Constable Jayman gazes up at the downtrodden house. They have had a number of reports about this house and he has been assigned to "keep an eye on it." Well so far he has patrolled this area several times and seen not so much as a speck of light through the barred windows. He notices that in the last few hours, someone has graffitied across the door, a warning sign blaring out to the whole street. Jayman looks worriedly across the road, towards the park. It is not a word he wants the children to read. Maybe he could ring the doorbell see if the elusive Krill is home. See if maybe, despite the rumours, it will turn out to be a non-threatening entity living in there. Someone who wouldn't mind painting over that word before the children see it. Jayman's hands actually tremble as he reaches forward, his hands trying to avoid the sprayed word, nervous about meeting the person who has been branded a "murderer" by the accusing red paint.

Aaron Fletcher is called shortly after Claire has stormed out. He is still sitting, still stunned, amid the shards of crockery. He can hear his mobile ringing but doesn't really care. Fletcher doesn't feel like moving. His mind is still going over the argument, trying to figure out what he had said wrong. Had he said anything wrong? He was just trying to shield her for fuck's sake! Just trying to show he cared about her, that he loved her. He was just trying to protect her. What had he said that implied any different to that? Why did she do this to him? Fletcher's phone continues to ring, distracting him from his marriage. He feels a gleam of hope it could be Claire ringing, maybe she realises that she overacted and is calling to apologise. Yes, it could be Claire. Fletcher springs out of his seat and begins hunting for his phone. It could be Claire.

But then he pauses, one couch cushion held high in his hands. Does he actually want to talk to Claire now? After what she said? She could just be calling to yell at him some more. Fletcher can picture her now, she is probably in her car pulled in at a petrol station. So angry she can't focus on her driving and wanting to yell at him over and over before hanging up. Typical childish behaviour of her. No, maybe he doesn't want to talk to her, maybe he didn't do anything wrong. The phone pauses for a moment as the answer phone kicks in, then begins ringing again. Someone definitely wants to talk to him. A cold shiver runs down his spine. The last time someone had so determinedly rung him like this, they had found another … Finally he finds the wretched device and presses answer.

CHAPTER ELEVEN

K ain hears the doorbell ring and freezes mid-click, heart pounding. Looking up the dark, dank stairs, the bare light bulb illuminates his deep red scar and sallow features. Is someone trying to break in? Kain grips the machete tightly and swallows the urge to flee. He waits. The doorbell rings again, he wishes that they would just go away. He does not want to see anyone, not until it isn't safe. It will never be safe. The doorbell rings again, a voice calls through the letter box.

Go away, go away, go away, go away.

The police have questioned nearly 10,000 people in connection with the murders, have searched around 30,000 vehicles and 8,000 homes. Nothing. So maybe they are frustrated and, of course, angry, so maybe they could be forgiven for the zeal with which search the house. Everything is documented and photographed, everything. No rotten, festering garbage bag is left untouched. It doesn't take them long to find Isobel Hilarie's wallet on the dresser upstairs.

Elizabeth sits in the interview room, revelling in her role as hero of the hour, a smile plastered across her wrinkled features. In fact, the whole police station has a lighter, happier feeling to it. We have got him! It's all over, we are safe again. We have done it! Except in one small dark corner, where Bullface sits nursing a hangover, pretending to supervise. This whole situation is leaving a bad taste in her mouth and she doesn't know why.

Fletcher thinks it is all wrong. He can almost see inside Elizabeth's mind. He has been here before with witnesses. They start saying things like, *"I knew it, I knew he was a bad man, it was a just a feeling."* It's what they will babble into the waiting microphones, smirk into television cameras. They want to be a hero, to be appreciated by an entire city for stopping a bad guy. Which is fine except it means that that witness becomes almost … contaminated. The witness begins to exaggerate, trying to create a stronger case, trying to justify their actions. The witness then starts to lose their credibility, loses their objectivity, in their ambition to become a hero they forget just who they are sacrificing. But then of course, this guy did have Isobel Hilarie's wallet on his dresser, that will take some explaining.

"I knew he was no good, ever since I met the man, I knew he was no good. I told my husband that he better watch that boy. He thought I was crazy."

Fletcher gives a forced smile as if to deny the very notion. It is enough to encourage Elizabeth Mitchell to continue.

"I monitored his comings and goings, you know." She waves a pad of paper at Fletcher. "You see, every time he went out, one of those poor girls died." Her voice drops theatrically with woe. Fletcher inwardly grimaces, Bullface slowly takes the notepad from Elizabeth with a barely audible thanks. Elizabeth's face changes slightly, put out by the officer's lack of interest in what she is saying. She is meant to be a hero! The officers should be thanking her.

"I heard him yelling one night. Just after that Taylor girl died. He was yelling at someone through one of those darn mobiles."

"What was he saying, Mrs Mitchell?"

"It's what first got me suspicious of him. Never have I heard a man so angry in my life, even my husband was shocked. It takes a lot to shock him, you know, he used to be in the army."

"What was he saying, Mrs Mitchell?" Fletcher repeats, slightly annoyed.

"He kept yelling about how it wasn't his fault." Ah finally, Elizabeth has the attention she was looking for.

They will interview his boss. The flabby man will sit there, jammed between the armrests telling them how hard it is to get good help these days. With a smile that sickens young girls, he will tell them just what a quiet guy he is, a quiet loner. Keeps mainly to himself, talks a lot about heavy metal, a kinda angry guy. The quiet, angry loner, well to tell you the truth, he will whisper, "I suspected the guy myself but I just didn't think." In the boss's mind he has already replaced the guy, perhaps with Lisa. Lisa the girl who wears thongs behind the counter, his tongue explores his teeth thoughtfully. Lisa could definitely do with some extra shifts. In his excitement he is not quite listening to Fletcher, only offering a mindless, "Yes, yes." That John guy is now history. Don't let the door hit you where Satan split you.

His name is John by the way. John Roberts. The only person who is surprised that he has been arrested is John himself. Everyone Fletcher interviews says the same thing. *"John is a quiet loner. I am not surprised, Officer. I suspected him myself but didn't think the kid would really..."* Even his girlfriend isn't helping. Bullface has listened in partial disgust as his girlfriend drones on and on about how she met him at a bad point in her life, how she has been longing to leave him for weeks and weeks now but she is just (lip quiver) so afraid (tissue dabbed at heavily made-up eyes) of his moods and what he would do to her (more lip quiver). She is John's main alibi but keeps saying how he wasn't with her the whole time, or she doesn't remember him being there that day or that she woke up during the night and he wasn't there.

Only John's mother actually sticks up for him. Well, kinda. She laughs outright at Bullface's hints. "My son might be a dirty, worthless slob, Officer, but he wouldn't hurt anyone, doesn't have the balls."

For some people, being arrested is a relief. The pressure of not being caught, of not having to hide every little thing. The constant looking over the shoulder, it gets a little too much. Some people subconsciously might let themselves be caught, becoming sloppy and unfocused because it's all too much to keep hiding. Some people want the opportunity to boast, it almost kills them trying to hold back the gloating, the *"Look how well I did to keep you occupied for so long."* Then for some people being caught is a surprise and they think they can talk their way out of it, they are the victim for being arrested. They try to manipulate their interviewers into seeing things their way. The woman was asking for it. I didn't see the light change. Most try and play innocent though, the trick really is to wear them down, keep going over and over the situations waiting for something to give, waiting for the sigh to say they have given up. That is what makes a good interviewer. Too many detectives give up quickly, thinking this guy isn't going to crack. They look for more DNA evidence, more little things that are hard to explain, thinking that they should leave the guy to stew. No, Fletcher thinks, you should never leave the guy to stew, if he is guilty then he will be busy thinking just how to explain the little things that are hard to explain. Fletcher prefers to drill over and over, letting other officers find the hard-to-explain items. If they find something, well good, something to shock them with, catch them off guard, break down the now drilled defences.

Fletcher didn't think today would end with him sitting opposite the guy, the guy they have been trying to catch for almost a year now, well eight, nine months. Actually, Fletcher isn't quite sure that this is the guy. Calm down, he keeps trying to tell himself, think through this rationally. Fletcher is still trying to calm down from the argument with Claire, keeps resisting the urge to check his phone under the table, in hope that she has already texted or even called him. Why hasn't she already? No, he is allowing himself to be distracted, he can't fuck this one up, no one in the station would forgive him. He can almost picture Bullface scowling at him through the glass, get on with it, she would be muttering. No, he has to do this calmly, rationally (oh why the fuck can't she be rational for once?).

Fletcher is a little disappointed though. He was expecting a suave handsome guy, someone worthy of him. This killer has got the better of him for a long, long time and Fletcher was expecting something more than the loser sitting in front of him. But then maybe that's what this guy's problem is. He is a loser wanting to be better than everyone else. But still, the greasy ponytail, the monobrow is not what he expected from a sophisticated, highly talented killer.

John Roberts is a rock man. He lives, breathes and eats his music. He is one of the greatest living rock gods of all time ... in his own mind. In reality his drum kit is dusty and he barely knows how to play. In conjunction with his job as a video clerk, he writes fantastic hair-raising reviews for a rock magazine – a magazine with a distribution of three thousand and falling. He spends his spare nights scrutinising forthcoming rock bands with names like *Two Doves are a Raven*, *V=New Shoes!* and *My Anus Itches*. In his mind he still has potential and he conforms to this image by always wearing a heavy black trench coat and biker boots, even in the summer. As a result he gives off a strong earthy scent, which his soon to be ex-girlfriend absolutely despises. Later, officers will argue that the realisation that he couldn't live up to what he wanted to be, the realisation that he is a nothing, could have been one of the many triggers. They will argue that they were seeking a man who seemed to be killing mainly for the power, the power over the city, over women. A man seeking such power would have so little in his own life, which was certainly true. Fletcher would argue that this man just didn't feel like the killer, an argument which even to his own ears is weak. Maybe the officers are blind-sided, just wanting to catch a killer, maybe they think Fletcher is trying to prolong his time in the spotlight.

Fletcher is aware though, of how desperately the other officers want this man to be the killer. He has read too many cases where officers have stereotyped certain offenders, almost blocking them into the role they want them to play. No one is innocent under constant scrutiny and there are always unexplainable clues. Maybe these officers are stereotyping the quiet loner too quickly but then maybe, knowing this, Fletcher is too reluctant to see the clues that are really there.

John is glaring at him now, his scariest glare which makes him look like a cross little child. Fletcher just can't take this seriously. There is no way this loser could kill all those women. Someone taps on the window, impatient for him to start the interview.

Fletcher clears his throat, typically he would try and minimise the offence, downplay the seriousness of the situation but that really doesn't apply here – *"Oh, don't worry you have only killed a few women, you are looking at six months at the most, maybe a little community."* Fletcher isn't the type to manipulate the suspect's self-esteem either, he just doesn't have it in him. He asks John to confirm the basic details and explains why he is here. John grunts answers but mostly he seems a little stunned.

Fletcher tries pinning him with his best, *I know what you did* look. It is ineffective. He wishes Bullface was in the room, she is the better intimidator. He tries to explain to John how futile it is to deny the charges. He says something along the lines of how he wants to hear John's side of the story.

John's arms spring from being crossed defiantly to hands slammed onto the table, beating in time to an angry scream. "No! No! No! You are not going to pin this shit on me," John snarls.

Two officers rush in eager to restrain him. Fletcher waves the officers back, trying to prove that he still has some kind of authority.

"Well you need to start talking." Fletcher makes his voice sound tougher, more authoritative tries to give off the impression that he is the man, the man who will listen. Behind the glass window, someone snorts with laugher, luckily unheard by John.

"What's in the safe, Mr Roberts?"

"What safe?"

There is definitely confusion in John's eyes but then Fletcher has been fooled before, by more convincing liars. The laugh has annoyed him, he wants everyone to know that he is still capable of doing his job just fine thank you. How dare they laugh at him, just who is back there?

"The safe."

"What safe?" John Roberts practically growls through clenched teeth.

"The safe in your kitchen." Fletcher fixes him with a knowing look. John Roberts still looks very confused.

"I don't have a safe."

"Our officers are working on opening it now." Fletcher tries his best *it's futile to deny* tone, straining his ears to try and catch another laugh. He sits back and crosses his arms.

John Roberts still looks very confused, thinks that he has been arrested by a complete fruit loop. This has to be some kind of joke. He doesn't know anything about the safe; he had inherited the house from his grandfather Arnold Mitchell, Old Arnie being slightly paranoid of his neighbours had hidden his most precious items in the safe. Old Arnie had died from Alzheimer's and had forgotten to tell his dearest it was there. Officers will work for an hour trying to jam it open, breaking through the rust only to find several faded nudie magazines and a gold wrist watch.

"I don't have a safe," John growls again.

Fletcher looks at him again trying to stare him down, angry eyeball meets angry eyeball. Fletcher tries to picture this face being the last one that stared down at a woman taking her last gasping breaths, but just can't see it. Behind the glass, the other officers are becoming more and more convinced that this is their killer, after all aren't they looking for a sociopath? Someone who is cool and calm, a good liar. Someone with a cruel streak, they are convinced that John is playing Fletcher. Fletcher being the trusting idiot is completely falling for it – hook, line and killer.

John is still trying to figure out why he is here. At first he thought it was a joke. Plenty of people are jealous of a cool guy like him and would love to ruin him. Plenty of people! John knows the old bat across the road has been watching him too. She could be the type who would be out to get him, she has already tried to organise a petition to get him out of her neighbourhood. She claims that he devalues the property. It's just a few rubbish bags, it's no big deal, they are just jealous that's all. Yes, he thinks, I bet it was her. It's her who should be the one sitting here, she is the one who should be arrested, after all if they found evidence in his house because of her ... well, excuse me, but isn't that something called breaking and entering? Let her be the one, he is just being victimised now. They are all out to get him, all of them, just because they are old and jealous. John's glare turns malicious as he thinks to himself, I am going to get her for this.

Fletcher catches the malevolent glare and feels uneasy. Even he can tell how badly this interview is going. It is time to prove himself, to dredge up every little piece of information or evidence, an onset of attacks. He needs to either prove John's innocence or guilt. Those people behind the door are listening, making notes. They are getting ready to pounce on his case, just waiting to prove his incompetence. Claire would love that; she would never let him live this one down. The kid is laughing at him too. Right it is time. No more Mister Nice Cop.

"Where were you on the evening of March 9th?"

"That was months ago, how am I supposed to remember?"

"Several witnesses reported seeing you that night."

"Good for them."

"They say they heard you yelling into a mobile that it was not your fault."

"So?"

"Well let's say that on that night, when you were heard

yelling over and over again that it wasn't your fault, a young girl lay dying, quite close to where you live."

John looks stricken for a moment then something seems to ting in his mind. Fletcher can almost see the light bulb flash. Whatever is coming next has to be an elaborate lie … or the realised truth.

"I was talking to my mother."

OK, that was a little surprising.

"What happened?"

"I had crashed her car. Some idiot rear ended me but she kept insisting that it was my fault, that I hadn't checked my mirrors."

"Were the police called?"

John snorts. Fletcher glares at him, annoyed. John is mocking him again. Those people behind the window are probably mocking him as well.

"The asshole drove off. What good would calling the police do?"

"Is there any evidence of the crash?"

"My mother will back me up," John says determinedly, unaware that she hadn't when interviewed earlier. Fletcher would have to interview her again.

"Of course there is the £500 bill from the mechanic," John continues with the bitter tone of someone who still really misses that five hundred.

"Which mechanic?"

"I don't know, my mother sorted it out." She didn't trust her son to find a good mechanic. He thought she had found the most expensive one on purpose.

"Where were you on Friday 21st August?"

"With my girlfriend."

"And she will be able to confirm this?"

"Well she and several hundred other people. We went down

to a festival for the weekend, drove her and two of her friends down." The girlfriend would confirm this, yes but quickly adding that she wasn't with him the whole time and she was pretty drunk. Given that this festival was being held over a hundred miles away from the city, it made for a pretty good alibi. The friends would kindly confirm that they left early on the Friday morning and came back late on the Monday evening, an alibi for both the murders of Adelina Sasha and Stella McQam, yes, but not a strong one.

"And where were you on Sunday 30th August?"

"In bed."

"All day?"

"Yup."

"Alone?"

"Yes."

The two men glare at each other, John has reverted back to his defences, reminding Fletcher almost of Jack Sasha. Maybe John had reminded Adelina of a younger Jack Sasha, maybe that's why she had gone with him. But then Adelina had been portrayed as sophisticated, elegant, she would not have gone for such a greasy young man. John doesn't seem like the type a girl like Fran Lizzie would trust either.

"I was at a gig the night before, we were out drinking till five," John sullenly admits. Gig or no gig, John did spend a lot of his weekends sleeping.

"On November 10th, a girl named Isobel Hilarie was murdered. Her purse was stolen."

John gives a half shrug, as if to say, "So?" But then his eyes suddenly widen.

"We found Isobel Hilarie's wallet in your bedroom." Fletcher smiles, try and talk yourself out of this one, punk. He sits back to watch the young man squirm, feeling suddenly quite triumphant. Maybe this would shock out a confession.

He doesn't know whether to be angry or happy. He has heard through the whispers that they have finally caught the bastard. He knows they haven't, of course. He doesn't particularly like being a bastard either, but oh well. He is angry because someone else is taking his credit, he has worked hard at this. It has taken years and years of fantasising and planning, carefully studying every inch of the city, surveying dump sites, of befriending police officers, subtly providing leading questions so he learns what corners to avoid, where the best CCTV is filmed. It has taken years to be this good and now some two-bit punk is taking it all away. He can feel the fear that engulfed the city retreating. Even his wife looked relieved earlier, all happy and smiling. That is definitely not allowed. She is talking about leaving the house, "to be social," wanting to join him in whatever he is doing – for the first time in months. That is definitely not allowed.

But then he is also happy. The fear is subsiding, people are taking chances again. While they believe that he is behind bars, he can hunt a lot more easily. People, well, women will look at him tonight with opening, welcoming smiles. Hell, they would be easy tonight, the months and months of stress of not being able to go out will mean one big crazy party tonight.

Brandi isn't invited. Brandi is never invited to anything and it just isn't fair. Mike Jones had promised to walk her home tonight. She had thought that they were getting along well and maybe, just maybe something was happening, but no. The news of the killer's capture had reached her office and Marcella had suddenly become the shiny, bubbly blonde, bouncing around the office talking animatedly about going out for a drink, and Mike had looked up and enquired what pub and maybe they could make it a group thing. The bitch already had a boyfriend!

It wasn't fair. They hadn't said, *"Brandi why don't you join us?"* Oh no, she was ignored. Mike was going for a night out with Miss Perfect, Miss Slender Thighs and Miss Bouncy. While Brandi has to walk home, alone in the rain. It isn't fucking fair!

"I can't believe you let a fucking killer go," the officer hisses at Fletcher, an hour after they have released John. Did the reporter hear that? Fletcher quickens his steps, appearing all the more guilty. The press are trailing the officers closely, hungrily demanding updates. Has the killer been caught? Who has been released?

Later, Fletcher would see the photo of himself, behind him stand several officers. Fletcher thinks they all look angry, like moments after the picture had been taken, they would have pounced. When the next body falls, Fletcher will be blamed by that same officer but at that point he will be beyond caring.

John Roberts was an asshole yes, but Fletcher knows he is not a killer. Not yet anyway. John is too easily angered to be a calm, precise killer. If John ever killed anyone, it would be someone he knew in a moment of anger. He is not the type to plan and hide, he is a striker. If John did kill someone he would be easily caught, he could barely clean up after himself let alone clear away a corpse. No, John's DNA would not match anything they had, Fletcher would put money on that if anyone would just listen to him. Fletcher believed John when he stammered that he had found Isobel's purse on the street close to the convenience store. Normally he would have just handed it in but he vaguely knew Isobel, had rocked out with her boyfriend, Frank, a few times and thought he would be seeing him again soon. Like the next night, but when Frank hadn't shown at the club it had ended up on his dresser, forgotten, work had been stressful and he had been drunk a lot lately. Frank would grudgingly confirm most of this – although this casual interview ruins any molecule of friendship between Frank and John. It gives Frank a tantalising hint of who the murderer might be. Frank will be openly hostile whenever he sees John after this. Not that John will leave the house much.

John leaves the police station angry. Anger that increases as he listens to a voicemail from that pathetic twat of an employer. *"Oh, heard about your recent trouble with the police, we don't want that kind of image for the store, already on thin ice due to attitude..."* Bullshit and more bullshit. *"Will put the redundancy check in the post."* Fuck ... that stupid bitch has ruined everything. Rage just swells through his body as he stomps home, unaware of what is following him. He is his own tornado of fury.

"Excuse me, do you have the time?"

She pauses and looks down at her watch. That pause is all he needs; striking, ripping across her throat and stepping back as she falls. He is well practised now, has this down to an art. She looks up, locking eyes as she falls. He smiles down at her then kneels and picks up her left hand. Slips off her watch and then begins to cut. There is just enough time to cut and listen to her choke and burble. She doesn't die instantly. He leaves thinking that it won't be long, just a few more seconds, he is in a hurry, has just enough time to prove to the city that they are wrong and stupid. Quickly, he turns his jacket the right way round, the little blood splats safely hidden ... not that anyone ever looks that closely. No one is around to see.

It's mid-December and extremely cold, the woman is still alive, still clinging on. It's going to be Christmas soon, she wants to live so badly, she has three young daughters and just wants more time. The cold is keeping her alive, slowing down her heartbeat but it's not enough. An off-duty paramedic finds her and rings for an ambulance. But it is not enough. It is enough though, for the reporters who say that she was taken to hospital alive. It is enough to scare him for the first time.

CHAPTER TWELVE

E lizabeth Mitchell is livid, absolutely lived. She has just seen John storm into his house, heard the loud slam of his broken door, it sent shivers pacing across her skin. The police have let him go? After what he did to those poor girls? Her hands wrinkle into tight fists. They have let him go despite all her evidence? All those hours of watching were for nothing. After all she had risked going into that house, despite what she had seen in his bedroom, they let him go? How could they?

She is alone tonight; he could easily come for her. She won't be able to protect herself against him. If those younger, stronger girls couldn't do it, what chance does she have? Maybe she should call her husband and ask him to come home, but he would be no match for that murderer. Maybe she should call her son, he would laugh at her of course but maybe if she told him what had happened, maybe he would come over for a bit, maybe even invite them to stay with him for a while. Just a little while, surely it wouldn't take long for the police to come to their senses and arrest him again.

Her hands shake as she reaches for the phone, out of habit

her other hand reaches for the blind. The phone smashes into the floor before she has even begun to dial.

Looking at her from across the road, from his own window, he stands watching in the dark.

Most people don't expect to die. These people don't close their eyes and peacefully slip away. Inconsiderately they keep their eyes open, staring at those around them with astonished or accusing eyes. This is especially true of those who die suddenly or violently. They stare directly at you, Fletcher decides, blaming you. Mrs Donaghue especially had a questioning stare, a frozen expression of accusation. The officers around him are also shooting reproachful glares his way. Angry mutters occasionally buzz like wasps directed at him, just slightly out of his hearing, as they move around Mrs Donaghue photographing and swabbing. One officer is now lifting her left hand so Fletcher can see and so that another officer can photograph, the rushed angry red scratches that formed the number 38.

Thirty fucking eight.

Thirty fucking eight. Number 39 might be Claire. Maybe he deserves it. He failed to protect Mrs Donaghue, maybe now he should be punished. Maybe of all the people in the world, he deserves to be punished. Maybe he should know how it feels to really lose a loved one to violence. This is the price of failure. Thirty fucking eight. Fuck he is tired. He is fucking trying, OK, and he just needs you to stop fucking staring.

Mrs Donaghue's blue eyes, just like Claire's eyes, seem to fixate on him. He, the bastard, had stood over her just like how Fletcher is standing now. If only Fletcher could see what she had seen, right now he would give up everything just to see what she has seen.

She had been on her way home from a pre-Christmas party,

the first of the season. She was dressed in a glittery silver number, festively tinted with red jewellery and ... her thick black leather gloves meant that there would be absolutely nothing under her nails belonging to the killer, even if she had fought against him. (Why couldn't they catch a fucking break?) The evidence seems to be showing she was caught unaware just like the others. He is smooth. He could stop a girl innocently in a city where everyone is going crazy. He must be handsome, but a trustworthy handsome.

They had done all they could but Kim Donaghue died on the way to the hospital. They had let the killer go, hadn't they? He had been allowed to leave, as angry as hell, No one is blaming you, Fletcher – wait no, everyone is blaming you, Fletcher. This seemed a rushed, fast kill and not a well thought through kill. The kind of kill Fletcher thought John Roberts was capable of, isn't that what he had been thinking when John left the station and now...? No, this was a well-planned kill. No one had been around to hear any attempt at a scream. It was fast but he was careful. He must have been waiting around for someone like her, just waiting in the shadows. It was fucking December, too many people in hats and dark clothes – thick, concealing coats. Too many people with their heads down, rushing to be somewhere.

They had even less evidence than usual. She had been alive when found. Instead of officers looking over every little detail on the scene, paramedics had trampled through it all. Instead of the photographers documenting every little detail, her clothes had been cut off in an attempt to revive her. They were investigating her now, hours later, looking for any small trace. Anything now was likely to be contaminated but it would be a start. It would have been worth it had she survived. But instead she had slipped away at the hospital, just to spite him. Had she died with her eyes closed but someone opened them? Or, or ...

why is he focusing on the fucking eyes. Where the fuck is Bullface? Bullrush? Bullface! He really needs to focus, needs to get away from the scolding eyes. He needs to talk to the off-duty paramedic, which will be hopeless but he still needs to. He needs to have a shower. He needs to go Christmas shopping. He needs to get away from the woman whose kids are expecting her home. He needs to get the fuck together and get some sleep. Man up. Thirty fucking eight. It is just a joke now, isn't it?

"Where have you been? I have been looking all over for you," Fletcher mutters. Truth be told, he hasn't been looking for Bullface, the last thing he wants is another fucking critic.

"I have been going over the evidence from the previous murders." She has been staring at the faces of the women young enough to be her daughter and nothing else.

"Anything?" Please don't let him have missed something, he would be lynched at this point.

"Nothing." Bullface's voice is laced with defeat.

"Do you think he targeted Shannon Leona on purpose? Knowing she was a cop, knowing it would damage the people investigating the case? Destroy morale and such?"

"It is possible, she was a visible cop most of the time. Lots of the public knew her."

"So maybe we should look at questioning those who knew we would be searching? It was a planned attack, wasn't it?"

"Great idea. Since it was announced on the radio and the television it will only be, what, a hundred or so people..."

"It was just a fucking suggestion. Have you got anything better?"

"Calm down."

"We need to do more; the press is all over the fact that the

CM THOMPSON

police released a suspect on the same fucking day a mother of three was killed."

"What did they want us to do? Arrest an innocent man because his neighbour is an interfering old bat?"

Fletcher never thought he would see the day when Bullface called a member of the public anything even remotely disrespectful.

"Are we even sure he is innocent?" Shit, Fletcher is even starting to doubt his decision. "Hundreds of people can't be wrong, can they?"

"The officers I had tailing him confirmed he went straight home. He spent the night blasting rock music, drinking and stomping around his living room before passing out." The officers hadn't seen the brief moment when Elizabeth Mitchell had peeked out of her window to see an angry John Roberts glaring at her, they had unfortunately seen him turning and mooning her. Bullface thought there will be a better time to tell Fletcher about that.

"You had officers tail him?" Why hadn't he thought of that? Fuck, he is messing up. But he doesn't trust the other officers anymore anyway they are just out to get him.

"I thought it would be wise to keep an eye on him and his neighbour."

Bullface still has his back even though she wouldn't say it. Fletcher gives a dry half-hearted laugh, some of the anger balled in his stomach subsiding.

"Fill me in on Kim Donaghue," she says and there it is, back again.

He is worried. For the first time since he started killing, he is worried. He is listening to the news report that the woman has been taken alive to the hospital, he is worried. She had seen him, hadn't she? Looked straight in his eyes as she crumpled. He is going home now, to shout at his wife then blame the Christmas stress. Stupid cow will believe him. She is too stupid to put anything together. The stained coat is going in the bin. He never liked it anyway. His wife had brought it on sale, sale! He is worth more than that! He will blame the Christmas pounds if she says anything. Not that he gains anything at Christmas, not like her. He sits, watching, waiting for an update, trying not to seem too eager. Hell, nothing wrong with seeming too eager. He can just say he is hoping she will survive. Most people are glued to the sensation eagerly, aren't they? He is just part of the masses. Finally an update, she is dead! Thank Santa, she is dead! But then ... what if ... what if she is still alive and this is how they are protecting her? No, they wouldn't have shown her sobbing brats on the news if she had lived. They wouldn't have put the children through that. He might have but they wouldn't. The bitch's throat was cut, there was no way she could have said anything. She is dead now. Dead and dissected. He has other work to do. He should have done two tonight, taken advantage of their relief, it is too late now.

It is supposed to be a friendly. A little match to help relieve some of the stress. Perhaps even work away a few unwanted pounds before the engorging Christmas season. Fletcher wants to play because his mind will not shut up. He is being driven insane by hundreds of voices whispering problems, advice and criticisms. A thousand nagging mothers-in-law all proclaiming quite simply *I told you so.* Fletcher just wants a break, a few hours of running up and down after one simple little ball. A chance to clear his head.

It is supposed to be a friendly. Just some of the police force, the lads playing against other lads. Fletcher knows just about everyone on this pitch, everyone knows him. Drank with him on special occasions, spent hours endlessly discussing every single aspect of the winning games. He has spent the last five years of his life playing friendlies against these lads. Usually a friendly means a friendly.

Fletcher has already had his ankle kicked, Joe accidentally kneed him in the back and Mark trod on his hand. Fletcher suspects that one of his own team was responsible for the stomach blow which leaves him dry retching for nearly a minute. "I am sorry, mate," is beginning to sound like an insincere chorus. Fletcher isn't even sure what is keeping him on this pitch as their piñata. Whatever it is, it is urging his tired, beaten body to keep running, despite all the muscular protests. He can hear Joe's footfalls pounding behind him, slowly catching up. Joe seems to be incensed by the rag-tag row of supporters, screaming for blood from the sidelines. Fletcher can't even see where the ball is anymore. He just seems to be running away from the fate behind him.

Should he just give up now? Why is everyone so angry at him today, he can't send an innocent man to prison, what good would that do? He can't make evidence magically appear that isn't there. He can't do anything; they can't do anything. Except kick him further down into the mud. Fletcher can't hear Joe anymore, he is hoping that somehow he has run far enough to be out of the game, just to take a quick breather. That's all he needs, just to breathe for a few ... the whistle blows from a far off right corner as the ball sails past his head. Fletcher turns to run away from it just as Joe lunges forward, knocking him down into the freezing cold mud.

"Foul."

"Sorry 'bout that, Fletch."

"Fletch?"

Oh just fuck off.

"What happened to you?" They haven't spoken in days. Fletcher wasn't even expecting Claire to be home.

"I tripped."

"Well, I am not washing those filthy clothes."

Christ, Claire isn't even going to let him through the fucking door without starting. Why has he bothered coming home? Why is he bothering with anything? He spent part of his day interviewing people who were as dumb as monkeys and twice as curious. The paramedic had seen nothing more than a shadow retreating in the dark. He was more concerned with trying to save Kim Donaghue. More concerned with doing the impossible, what if it had been someone else? What if they gave Kim up for dead and went running after the bastard? Everything would be different then, wouldn't it? The bastard would have been caught. No, he can't think that way. Shit, he just needs to get through the door in peace. Take some aspirin; put some more ice on his knee. But no, Claire has to be there, waiting.

"Aaron?" Fletcher doesn't recognise his own name for a minute, he is Fletcher to everyone but Claire. He tries to swallow the growing anger, he doesn't want another shouting match, not now.

"Claire," he says finally. "Don't worry, I will wash them."

"I think we need to talk."

Shit!

CHAPTER THIRTEEN

Christmas arrives subdued and dark. Some greet it with relief, any excuse to try and forget what is going on. Some greet it with anger. It was spring when Fran Lizzie Taylor's discarded body had been found, they still haven't got anywhere. No leads, no real evidence, nothing. All due to incompetence. The police don't know their ass from their elbow. They hadn't even found the other bodies. Everyone knows that there are other bodies. It has leaked out that Kim Donaghue was branded with a number 38. Fran Lizzie was been 22. It doesn't take a cop to make a connection. They had only found six bodies! Six out of sixteen or thirty-eight! Fail! The police are failing. The police don't even know if there is one killer or more. The amateur detectives think there are at least two, maybe even three. They might all be working together. That would explain how they are able to overpower so many different women. Why are the police only looking for one man, not three? Why haven't more details been released? They could help if they knew more. Why could the cops on TV catch a man within half an hour but these fucking useless guys are taking well over a year? Security is at an all-time high this Christmas. Security locks are selling as fast as they can be ordered. No one is going anywhere alone. Bosses are encouraging everyone to take taxis home from Christmas parties and even then, two people at least in the taxi. More houses go up for sale; more people go to the in-laws for Christmas and never come back. It won't last. People always value convenience over safety; they will start to relax again eventually. It's taking longer and longer to recover after each one now. They know there will be a next one.

Brandi Parr is having an insufferable Christmas. She is back to being the office weirdo again. She hasn't had so much as a Christmas card from Mike Jones and he had spent the Christmas party locking eyes with Marcella. Slut! He is walking her home every day now, has been since Kim Donaghue's murder. Bet they are doing more than kissing under the mistletoe. What was it going to take for her to be noticed?

To make it worse, her sister has invited everyone over to her mansion. "You don't want to spend Christmas alone, sis." Yes, yes, she does want to spend Christmas alone. Alone, away from her mother and her constant "helpful" tips. Her sister will insist on giving them a tour of her massive, luxurious house and her mother will insist on giving Brandi nose-hair trimmers for Christmas. Her sister's man will be irritating. Her mother should be giving him the nose-hair trimmers.

Kain has been saving the last of the turkey-flavoured noodles for Christmas and sits slurping down the warm strands eagerly. He had wanted to order in a few special things for the occasion but the door bell has been ringing a lot lately, and he can't face going upstairs just yet. Not while he still has cigarettes, coffee and an internet connection. Why did they keep coming? How did they even know? Kain is not enjoying Christmas, well hasn't enjoyed Christmas in a few years. But now, this one is the worst one. Even Kain has heard now about the murders, has spent days frantically searching the internet for more information – all the more reason to stay down here. But then is it really safe down here? The cooling remains of the noodles are abandoned for the twentieth cigarette of the day. Fear sets in again and Kain begins frantically assessing and replanning escape routes out of the house. Should he stay in the cellar? It feels like the safest room, no windows for people to break through. It would be the last place anyone would think to look, the cellar's door is almost completely camouflaged. If anyone did break in, Kain would hear their footsteps upstairs and have enough time to ... but what if they saw the cellar door and came downstairs first. There is nowhere to escape to if they did that. Maybe Kain could hide somewhere down here, the cellar is dark, lit only by computer-screen glare. But then how hard is it to remain quiet and hidden? They could be in the house for a long time, waiting ... what if they lit a fire? There would be no escaping but then upstairs, upstairs ... can't go upstairs. But the disused kitchen, that has cupboards, doesn't it? Or would that be the first place they looked? They could already be watching the upstairs couldn't they?

No, an inner voice tries to soothe, it's OK, no one is watching, that's crazy talk. It's OK, no one knows we are here. It's OK. We are safe. I am safe here. I am safe here. I am.

Bullface has no time for Christmas. She had asked her sons to decorate and they have, technically, if putting two strands of tinsel on the tree was decorating. They knew they were getting gift vouchers anyway. They have never really been a Christmas family, not since the boys were little. Bullface and her husband had agreed not to do presents. He understood exactly why she wasn't feeling very Christmassy and to be fair, it wasn't as if Bullface was easy to buy for anyway. She never liked anything he bought. He is actually quite happy to relax on the sofa and watch movies with the boys. Chewing chocolates and sipping a beer. Today and tomorrow would be the only days when he could be irresponsible.

Bullface has nowhere to go to escape. They have finished working on refurbishing their latest house but now have to sell it before buying another project. No one is buying right now in the city for some strange reason, everyone is trying to sell. She wants to give this house to the boys, just to get them away from her for a while. But they are still too young, they would kill each other before the last box was unpacked. Bullface is feeling a little frustrated. She really just wants to go somewhere and take her mind off everything. She just wants to spend a few hours away from the murders, away from Christmas. She can't just sit with the others and watch mindless nonsense. She isn't a relaxing type of person, can't switch off – can't go into work either. She has looked over everything to do with the case to the point that she can almost recite it. Bullface closes her eyes, they are missing something. There is nothing to tie these women together, they have nothing in common. They were just in the wrong place that is what is making things even more difficult. They can't warn anyone to take precautions because everyone is in danger. Everyone who is female.

2. Jane Doe 217
    Age 17–25 (estimated)
    Trauma to the left hand
    C.O.D – Unknown

She can clearly picture the Polaroid of a young woman, lying naked on the ground. The woman is covered in bruises and deep interlacing cuts, twisted jagged lines lay slashed across her throat. Her hands had been carefully placed across her chest, the palms face down, so that the number two so cautiously carved can be clearly seen. Is he still taking photographs? He couldn't be, could he? He could be. What trophies had he taken from her? Will they ever even find out who she was? They are trying. Yes, they are definitely still trying but then no one is missing her. No missing reports match her details. Possibly she was illegal, possibly she was a prostitute, possibly she had been homeless. She was young, possibly a runaway? No one recognises her, despite the reconstructed face, despite the carefully cropped picture from the Polaroid ... Polaroid? Who even had Polaroid cameras now? That would be a distinctive feature in the killer's house, wouldn't it? If only they could put out a news bulletin like that, police are searching for someone with a Polaroid camera. Jane Doe 217 was estimated to have been killed between two and five years ago. That means that he had been killing for a long time and they have only just noticed. That was the biggest disappointment, that they have only just noticed.

22. Fran Lizzie Taylor (March 9th)
    Age 22
    Number inflicted on left hand
    C.O.D – Throat cut

His first public kill. Killed around 1am, a near-instantaneous death. Bullface can still remember standing on the grass looking at the girl. She had been thrown over a fence. The first indicator that he is strong, stronger than most people. If they ever corner the guy, they can expect one hell of a fight. More caution needs to be shown if they are ever to apprehend another suspect. They cannot make a single mistake against this one. What else? He had taken her purse, hadn't he? He likes his trophies. More evidence if they should ever find him. Bullface thinks that he might live alone. Surely, if he lives with someone else, they will have noticed these strange comings and goings. They would have seen some kind of bloody clothing, maybe even an idea where he would be hiding these trophies. Unless, unless he really was working with someone. She doubts that now, only one person had ever been seen leaving the crime scenes, only one person on the fruitless CCTV. One dangerous person.

Number Not Known – Adelina Sasha (August 21st)
    Age 38
    Trauma to the left hand
    C.O.D – Throat cut
    Possible trauma inflicted to face, stomach and arms

Three of his known victims have been subjected to a prolonged attack, the others suffered quick near-instantaneous deaths. Is there something about these ones? Or is it merely time and opportunity? He had given them Jane Doe 217's picture with Adelina. He wanted them to know what he had done. Did just one photo mean that there had been only one previous kill before Fran Lizzie Taylor? Or had they missed other bodies? Did he do this purposely just to confuse them? Adelina had been found in the woods, a picnic spot. They have searched other picnic spots but the possibility of missing something is high, too much land, too much litter. No one wanted to be out in the woods after what happened to Shannon. He is doing this on purpose, to scare them, to confuse them, to taunt them ... to control them.

They don't even know what number Adelina was or if there had been a number. There must have been but not knowing what it was means the number sequence is harder to figure out.

28. Stella McQam (August 24th)
Age 37
Number inflicted on right hand
C.O.D – Stab to the heart

The stabbed-twice prostitute. She had been killed in a busy location, in an alleyway in a busy location. Not like anyone was really going to look too closely at what a man and a woman were doing in an alleyway, were they? Not unless she had screamed her head off. Even then ... large amounts of DNA found at the scene but nothing useful. So many dead ends on this one. So much time wasted checking alibis. Should have just arrested everyone who was a DNA match, they were all guilty of something anyway.

Had he taken a trophy from Stella? It is likely. She hadn't been carrying much on her but then girls these days weren't. Too many men eager to take everything. She had probably hidden her takings and personals somewhere. Her friends said she hadn't left anything with them, but then that was relying on their honesty ... then there is that business with the *Missing* poster. DNA showed that the cigarette stubbed out on the poster was from Stella ... but they hadn't found any cigarettes or a lighter on her. Had he taken her cigarettes as a trophy? Or had she merely got the cigarette from her last customer?

Stella is number 28, Fran Lizzie is 22. Doesn't take a genius to see what is going on here, did it? But then their search for more had led to...

30. Shannon Leona (August 30th)
    Age 29
    Number inflicted on left hand.
    C.O.D – Exsanguination
    Trauma inflicted across the body

Shannon had been knocked unconscious by a blow to the head. A scrape of gravel indicated it was a rock from the scene of the abduction. The bastard had been there with them, waiting for someone to move away from the herd. Had he been someone helping them? Or had he just known about the search because of the bloody media and took an opportunity? They had to be seen doing something by the public, yes, but maybe broadcasting exactly what they were doing had been a mistake. It had stopped them searching even more in the woods, hadn't it? Was that what he wanted? Had Shannon stumbled onto something incriminating?

Did he know Shannon? Did he know Adelina? Was that why their attacks had been more brutal? Shannon didn't seem like the type to cheat, but then ... he had really beaten her. Bullface has seen the autopsy report. Cause of death – exsanguination, blood loss. A frenzied kill, multiple stab wounds just like Adelina – well what they guessed had happened to Adelina. Why? Why inflict that much pain? Had it been opportunity? Why hadn't anyone seen Shannon being carried away? Why did it take them so long to realise she was missing?

Shannon seems like a personal kill but then this killer, he likes to play them, doesn't he? Takes what he can get to keep them guessing. He had taken a trophy from Shannon too, hadn't he? They thought he had taken her purse but no, Robbie had found that in their car later on. He took something else, something much more personal.

34. Isobel Hilarie (November 11th)
   Age 19
   Number inflicted on left hand
   C.O.D – Throat cut

Their youngest known victim, the drunk girl who was an easy kill. The girl known as Sir Izz the Mad, who carried a wallet not a purse because she was Sir Izz. The girl covered in beautiful bright drawings of aliens, butterflies and dinosaurs. The girl who only wanted some chocolate and not to get her throat cut. Back to the throat slices, he seemed to like that method. It was convenient. Speaking of convenient, did she die because she seemed like an easy kill – she looked drunk in the CCTV footage – or had he been stalking her, waiting for the right moment? Stalking certain victims would explain the time lapses between kills, but no one had noticed anyone following these women. How was he choosing them? Stalking took a lot of time as well, there was no way he could have been stalking both Madison and Isobel. Madison was meant to be in classes at the time she was killed, it had to be him choosing women at random. But he had arranged to meet Adelina, hadn't he? This killer definitely planned things. He would look for locations, look for opportunities. He probably already had a place picked out for the next and was just waiting for the fly. But then going back to the dismissed theory, what if there was two different killers? The stalker who killed Adelina, Isobel and Shannon, and then the opportunist...

Then there was the trophy he took from Isobel. They had thought he had taken her wallet. What a fiasco that turned into, if only John Roberts had handed that wallet in to the police or to the convenience store. Why did he have to recognise the face on the ID inside and take it home? Why did he have to give them a small hope that maybe they had finally gotten somewhere? Only to turn out to be another dead end, so many hours wasted on checking out a deadbeat. Now they need to keep an eye on John Roberts too. Now they have to deal with more people, too many people all jumping to the wrong conclusions. Why do people always have to blame the loner? Why do normal civilians have to get involved? Unless they are an eyewitness, she has no time for their "suggestions".

The killer had taken a trophy, he didn't waste that precious time looking for Isobel's purse but he quickly settled on something else. It had taken Bullface a while to figure out what, because they had all presumed it was a purse; they hadn't looked too carefully at the CCTV footage of Isobel. After the John Roberts fiasco, she went back to the CCTV again the video footage clearly shows Isobel entering the shop wearing a necklace. The footage is too blurry and small to make out what kind of necklace, but there is something there. Isobel was not wearing any jewellery when she was found. Bullface has practically interrogated the clerk to see if he could remember any more about it or if anything had been found on the floor that night. Nothing! Frank was too drunk to remember what his girlfriend had been wearing but her bedroom was filled with artsy jewellery. She wore something different every day. Bullface is certain that the killer has taken Isobel's necklace, they can't add even add that one to any possible search warrant, too vague.

36. Madison Albrook (November 11th)
   Age 20
   Number drawn on right hand
   C.O.D – Throat cut

Then there is Madison, this time they actually saw the killer. Bullface has watched that footage over and over, watching as the seemingly young couple appear on screen, she is clutching at his arm as if afraid or unable to support herself. They appear out of the bushes from the other side of the screen, the male purposely keeping his head down. He is dressed in a dark outfit and wearing a dark beanie. Bullface sees him in her sleep now, that dark black mass moving across the screen over and over, always abandoning her, throwing her down onto the memorial poppies. Only in her dreams he looks up.

They are still unsure on this one. Madison's number was done in felt tip, was it a very clever copycat? Or more likely was it because he knew how little time he had to act, or was it the second killer? They would know for sure if they found his trophy case, wouldn't they? So many unanswered questions, no wonder she couldn't turn her mind off and concentrate on Christmas, all these questions demand answers.

This murder had the most witnesses, that's what made this so frustrating. So many people saw a man waiting around, dressed in winter clothing. On Isabel's death, they had heard what they are presuming was the killer, as he phoned for an ambulance and now visual – useless visual. See the evil, hear the evil but still can't recognise that evil. So many men frequented the park dressed in dark winter clothing. People had said they thought someone was waiting around, reading the paper and drinking something. Well nothing found in any of the bins had DNA matching to a previous site, nothing matching to DNA found in the phone box. So much DNA and just not knowing which DNA was his. But then one slip up, one slip up and then there would be DNA linking some of the crimes.

That innocent man had been killed around this time too, the first of the fatal paranoid attacks. His wife had hit him with a golf club when he tried to sneak into his own home. Several other men had been beaten up on the streets just for looking at a woman the wrong way. They have increased the patrols as much as they can, but Bullface knows that these paranoid attacks will continue until they catch him. If they catch him? What had she said at the time of Madison's death? In that briefing?

"What we do know is that he has killed two victims in less than forty-eight hours, as Adelina Sasha was killed on August the 21st and Stella McQam on the 24th, now he has killed two victims in less than twenty-four hours. Something is making him speed up. These kills are well planned and well executed so it is unlikely that he is giving up. I think we can expect him to continue at this pace and he won't stop until he is caught." He seemed to like showing off. But nothing for nearly a month, had they made him slow down? Was he losing control? Losing opportunities? But then Kim had been number 38. Where is 37? Where is number 35? Had he killed three women in just one day? It just doesn't seem possible.

38. Kim Donaghue (December 4th)
    Age 35
    Number inflicted on left hand

C.O.D – Throat cut

Talking to Kim's husband had been hard. The fact she had been found alive was hard. If that paramedic had just been a few minutes quicker. It had been Kim Donaghue's first outing since her youngest, Emily, had been born. First time out in over a year. Kim had gone to meet some friends for dinner and a catch up. Her husband had said she was meant to take a taxi home, had promised him that she would take a taxi home. But then the restaurant had been too hot according to her friends. They hadn't finished catching up and thought that a little walk would be enough to help cool down, they were all going the same way after all. When they parted ways, Kim only had to walk three streets and she would be home. She managed a street and her friends didn't hear or see a thing.

He took her purse. He also took a mother away from her three children just before Christmas. What a fucking bastard. Bullface had to talk to those children, only one of them really understood what was going on. She had to face them and talk to them. They were Mr Donaghue's only alibi after all.

What did they really know about this killer?

Anna Stevenson had said she thought he was a young man, but what was young to Anna? Probably mid-thirties. They thought he was a jogger or a runner, knew he had met Adelina jogging. If he was a jogger that would explain why he had such detailed knowledge of the city. Bullface thought if they could get more CCTV footage then he would appear all over ... along with several hundred innocent joggers, walkers and runners. He had probably lived in this area for a long time though, they weren't looking for anyone transient.

They had heard a crackling whisper of his voice, nothing distinctive but it sounded like a man who was calm, not nervous at the chance of being caught, not apologetic for his actions – a sociopath.

He is looking for attention, he has been killing secretly for over four years before going public. His kills are elaborate, dramatic. He is working up to something, Bullface is sure of that, if he gets the opportunity it will be big. The victims have shown no sign of sexual assault (except for Stella and that was extremely unlikely to be him). Whilst he has a huge disdain for females, Bullface thinks that he is unlikely to be a homosexual. He is the type to get release from the targeting and the kill itself. Which is why he must be building up to something big. Maybe he has already chosen his next victim and his next kill site. The killer is playing them, tormenting and tantalising them. Bullface thinks that they should be suspicious of any leads from any of the cases. This killer is likely to play them, leave conflicting evidence on purpose, leave DNA on purpose – not his DNA of course.

They think he might be unemployed, maybe he has been made unemployed within the last year which could explain why his public kills have increased. If he has been fired by a female boss as well that could explain some of the disdain. If he is employed, his job would be not a regular 9 to 5. He operates during the night and during the day, which suggests a shift worker or someone who works from home.

Bullface thinks that he will be young; he is strong and very mobile. She will be very shocked if it is anyone over the age of forty. He has to have good looks, maybe not great looks, great looks would be noticed and remembered but he will have a harmless look to him. He would look average. He is a local. He is more likely to be found socialising with guys than girls. A guy between the ages of twenty-five and forty, good health, reasonably good looks, who works random hours or does not work at all ... oh and he owns a Polaroid. That should narrow the suspects down – maybe to a few thousand or so!

There is just too much they don't know, too many maybes. Bullface is tired of going over everything. Every time she analyses what she can, she comes up with a different answer, different explanations for this killer's behaviour. They can't be sure of anything.

Bullface feels suffocated by her thoughts, by the constant crunching sounds as her family grazes in front of the blaring television. She has to get out for a little while. Perhaps go somewhere to really, really think. Somewhere quiet and alone.

Fletcher is actually feeling quite relaxed. He has on a festive jumper (Claire didn't expect him to wear it) and has a drink in his hand. It doesn't matter that his in-laws are due to arrive any minute. It doesn't matter that he has bought Claire the wrong piece of jewellery – again! It doesn't matter that the Christmas turkey is burning in the oven. He is going to quit. They have decided on it. He is going to quit as soon as this case is over. He has sworn on his marriage. That day he came home from football and she had said those fatal words, "We need to talk." He had thought it was over completely. He thought she was going to ask for a divorce. She said that work was destroying him and he agreed. She said she was tired of arguing all the time. Things had been too tense and she was afraid and angry and stressed. He said he was tired of being blamed for everything and he was sorry he was stressed all the time. He said he found it hard to cope with the deaths of so many women and was only worried about her safety. Then they hugged and forgave each other and talked again about having children. He said that he was going to quit his job. She thought it was for the best. And now they are going to have a perfect family Christmas, with her parents, with no arguing or bickering. It is all going to be OK now because this is the Christmas Day special where all the dreams come true and everyone is happy. There aren't three little Donaghue girls wondering why their mother hasn't come home. She has just walked through the door with the most amazing Christmas story to tell them. They had caught the killer six months ago thanks to Fletcher's genius idea and everything is going to be just swell and dandy on this Christmas Day.

Robert Leona, the man who can't escape the nickname Robbie Bobbie even though he isn't a bobby anymore. Rob is spending the first Christmas in seven years without his wife, he had never even thought something like this could happen. He had always thought she would be by his side no matter what, for better, for worse. The tears threaten again. He is always on the point of tears these days – one of the many reasons he has to be alone. They are all worried about him, he knows that. Rob, for the first time since he was a teenager, has had to lie to his mother. He has told her that he is spending Christmas with some friends. To his friends, he said that he is spending Christmas with his parents. He had to lie to everyone, just to stop their worrying. They just didn't understand. They might call to check on him, lies have a way of exposing themselves faster than ... no, he can't dwell on the lies, he has to focus, has to make a decision.

That mousey woman, Jennifer, she is just like Shannon. Mouse on the surface, but lion at heart and look at what happened to Shannon. He has to protect Jennifer now, doesn't he? If he fails to protect another woman, then what good is he? But what Jennifer wants to do, that isn't right. He needs to talk her out of it. But then ... then ... Shannon's wedding ring has gone. Of all the things to take, he had taken her fucking wedding ring. Tears lit only by next door's Christmas lights run down his face. The bastard took her wedding ring...

Jack Sasha's house is empty and cold, it has been stripped to its bare bones. Fresh coats of plaster cover spots where furniture, flung in rage, had fire-worked across the room, then exploded into bursts of wood and wall. Everything he and his wife had worked so hard for has been destroyed. Every day he wakes up and destroys something else. It had started with her cup, then the plates, whose patterns he had hated but she had loved (or maybe she also hated, but she liked to make him mad). Then, just for the sheer satisfaction he bent the knives and forks into twisted memorials. He had built a fire in the garden, shit, after that one he was surprised that his neighbours hadn't called the police. Maybe they had decided it was closure or some other bullshit. The fire had helped a little, and now gone were the Christmas decorations, gone were the condolence cards and most importantly gone was the *Coping With Your Grief* book her mother had given him. He had sat and watched it all burn, relishing the heat, sipping a whiskey.

The anger still hasn't gone away. Christ he is allowed to be angry, isn't he? He saw what that bastard did to his wife. He'd made Anna Stevenson tell him everything she knew. Jack knows he should feel angry at his wife's infidelity but then he couldn't blame her. It's not like his eye had never strayed. She would have never left him Jack knows that, no matter how good this guy was, Adelina would never have left him. That bastard took her away.

What had he promised? *"I will find you, everything you did to her, I will do to you,"* right on the news. That bastard must have seen that, must be laughing at him now. But he means it; he will find this fucker.

When that mousey woman came to him at the funeral, he wasn't really listening to her but then, then he saw her plans. The mouse had brains. Jack is always too angry to think he knows that, but she could still think. He will take orders from her, to a certain point it could work for a while.

Jack is ready now. He has quit his job. ("You are welcome back anytime," his scared boss had said. "Just take all the time you need.") The stripped house is up for sale – hence the fresh coats of plaster, to hide the undesirable parts. Adelina's most cherished possessions have gone to her mother and the evidence of his rage has gone into the dustbin. The rage hasn't gone, oh no, it is buzzing around his head from the minute he awakes to the moment he passes out. Just a human stick of rage that's all he is now. Rage threatens to spilt him apart at the seams but it doesn't matter. He is ready. Every day he focuses on the training, the running, the punching bag, he is ready. Oh yes, he is definitely ready.

Jennifer Taylor keeps up appearances alongside her husband. They have to, have to be seen as being OK even if they aren't. It makes things awkward otherwise, more awkward than usual. You would think after ten months, people would be able to look her in the eye and talk to her. God knows what would happen if she actually showed how she is really feeling on the inside, instead of smiling and being polite, always pretending she is happy and in a better place. Happy? No, there is no happiness anymore, no peace, no joy. That plaster was ripped away when her daughter's throat … no, stay calm, composed. They only need to stay another hour, an hour will be sufficient. Then she can go back to her maps and plans. The thought that they are going to catch this bastard is the only thing keeping her going now.

They will catch him – if the police are just going to fail them, well then they owe it to the dead to find him. They have to do something; she can't keep watching the news and seeing another girl's face. Can't keep ringing only to be told, "No progress." They are going to go out and find him. It will take some work, it's not like he is obvious. She has tried to get more help, help from people she knew wouldn't talk her out of this. Mrs Hilarie had refused, Jennifer hadn't expected that – she'd just flat out refused, told Jennifer that she needed help, and then just walked away! She hadn't managed to talk to Ms Addison and then none of Stella McQam's family were reachable. Then there was Mr Donaghue, Mr Donaghue with his three young daughters. She couldn't ask him, he needed to be with his children. Mr Donaghue was the only one out of them who still had something to lose. This unfortunately means that it is just her, her husband and Jack. Maybe Robert Leona if he ever makes up his mind. She could ask other people, but then could she really ask her friends and family? She has to spend so much time already convincing them that she is not crazy, they will only try to talk her out of doing this, they don't understand her pain. She could ask strangers but then could she trust strangers? Fran Lizzie had trusted a stranger, hadn't she? Despite all those years of telling her not to. Only people like her husband and Jack know how it feels, how bad the pain is. Only people who have already lost have nothing left to lose. Stick with those people, she tells herself those are the only people she can trust.

Her mobile bleeps bringing Jennifer back into the world, her husband had been about to shake her, worrying about the people around them. She excuses herself to answer her phone to a message.

"OK, I am in. I have some friends I know will help."

Finally, a Christmas miracle!

Elizabeth Mitchell's house is pure Christmas for the grandchildren. Her family sit, joyously opening presents. Her husband happily photographing everything but Elizabeth doesn't feel a part of the Christmas joy. She tries to focus on the grandchildren and their happiness, tries to focus on the cooking and her own presents. Tries but her eyes only want to look at one thing – that house across the road. Her mind constantly worrying what is he going to do next.

John Roberts is still angry. He is angry at his pathetic now ex-girlfriend. He is angry at his magazine as it is ceasing publication, but he is angry most of all because his mother has decided to move into the house

"Just until this all blows over, Johnny."

"Johnny, how could you live in such filth?"

He hates being called Johnny, hates her sneers. His mother is never going to let this go. She is always going to be there, waiting for him to screw up again. He hadn't screwed up though. They had picked on him. They had broken into his house and gone through all his stuff. Then had the audacity to arrest him! Then that fucking hag had told his mother about the mooning. She fucking deserved it, if she was going to be watching him every second then she deserved to see his ass. Probably the most erotic thing the old bitch had seen in years.

"Johnny, I think it is best that I stay with you," his mother had said, after receiving that hysterical call. "I don't want you doing anything else stupid."

He might have been able to cope with that. He is not that stupid, he knows how dangerous anger can be, learnt that at his father's feet. He might, despite everything, be able to cope with his mother living with him. But why does she have to nag him every day, every damn day.

179

It started with the house. OK, maybe it was a little messy but it was just how he liked it. It was comfortable! The garbage bags on the lawn kept the old ladies muttering, it sent out a clear signal to them, a leave-me-alone signal. So what does his mother do? She rents a fucking skip. She cleans every bag, every rotting bag off the garden. She plants flowers ... FLOWERS in WINTER? How stupid can you get? She nags and nags about the state of the house. "If you don't clean this up, Johnny, I am going to clean this up." Like he is still a child! Well there was no way he was going to clean up after a comment like that was there?

He retreated to his bedroom, slammed the door and played rock music as loud as he dared. When he came out a few hours later, for something to eat, it had all changed. Gone were the whiskey bottles cluttering the stairs, he had been collecting those! Gone were the takeaway boxes (maybe he won't miss those). Gone was the dirty, stained but comfortable sofa, it was comfortable! Even the carpet had been pulled up. The walls had been scrubbed, really scrubbed. The kitchen was empty too. Instead of washing the mouldy plates, his mother had simply binned everything. Everything had gone into the skip. She was in the bathroom cursing and scrubbing. The towels had been thrown, the shower curtain had been thrown, everything else was being treated with a heavy dose of bleach. She was on a rampage.

"I am doing your bedroom next, Johnny," she warned. There was no way he was letting her into his bedroom but somehow she still got in. She threw out his trench coat. "It stinks, Johnny." She wanted to repaint the walls and make everything look nice. She decided to make herself comfy and put up tinsel. She put up a Christmas tree. She wanted to invite the hag across the road over for Christmas cake. "She needs to see you are not a monster."

John drew the line at that. Mrs Interfering Mitchell could stay in her cave and watch through her curtains (he knows she is still watching) but she was not ever coming back inside his house.

"You can't live like this, Johnny."

"Well, she will be dead in a few years, Mother."

His mother had not liked that comment at all, she had lectured him for nearly an hour over that comment, ending with the wish for the "good" old days when she could put him over one knee until he agreed with her.

John knows she is just waiting until after Christmas to do the talk. She is building up to something. Already she had suggested cutting his hair. *"You would look so smart without a ponytail."* She has suggested tweezers for his eyebrows, like he was a girl! A new year, a new you. No, no, no. She wanted to get him new clothes for Christmas, something suitable for interviews. He wanted to shit in a box and wrap it up, a special gift for his mother and Mrs Interfering Mitchell. He didn't have the balls to do that, only to think about it occasionally.

John has to put up with it, he has no choice but to grit his teeth and mutter. It isn't just Mrs Effing Mitchell watching him anymore. Everyone is watching. Everyone knows he had been accused. If he goes out, he is surrounded by reporters, by people wanting to know everything. He can't leave the house. Privately, he is relieved his mother is here, even though she is getting rid of his stuff. His mother being here means that no one will attack him, no one will ever go against his mother. Not even his father dared.

Well, she is cooking the turkey now and for once, it actually smells good. She might even force him to eat a vegetable. Maybe for now, he is OK with that. But that bitch across the road is still going to pay.

He is playing the perfect husband, has to reassure his wife after all. Don't want her getting suspicious, definitely do not want her confiding in her brother. They look like they have been whispering. He had given his wife some perfume for Christmas, perfume and jewellery, the cliché gifts that made her happy. He has also allowed his wife to live for a little longer. Greatest gift of all.

He wants to go out hunting, needs to get away from her disgusting relatives. They won't let him go out alone, he knows if he says he is going running, then her brother will join him "for a chat". It would be too obvious anyway if he goes out on Christmas Day and then another body bursts out onto the news. Not even his wife is that stupid. He really wants rid of that barnacle now. How can he get rid of her but not fall under investigation? If the police had a warrant and reason to search his home ... well he would be in deep trouble then, wouldn't he? The police are more efficient than his spying relatives.

He will just have to concentrate on planning what he is going to do next, instead of actually doing it. He needs to think through as much as he can. No room for a single mistake now, everyone is watching. He needs to do something big. Something fun!

Bullface told her family that she was going to a cold, draughty church. Somewhere she could offer prayers for the victims and be thankful for her family at Christmas. She could have said she was going stripping, under her code name Vixen and they would have still said, "Yes, Mum," barely hearing her.

She hadn't planned on going to see Pippa but here she is, alone in the graveyard. No one for miles around to hear her scream ... no, that's not true, there are other people milling around, everyone's heads are firmly down, all eye contact avoided. No one wants to strike up a conversation here. No one wants to make friends with new people at the moment, especially not here. Bullface thinks again about the girls, the victims. How on earth could he lure someone, get them to talk to him when everyone else is so scared of their own shadow? Why did he have such a power?

No, thoughts of the killer don't belong here in this graveyard. It isn't right this is a sacred place ... but then nothing is sacred to him. He seems to enjoy destroying everything sacred. He could even be in the graveyard right now, waiting for a vulnerable lone woman. "Bring it on, you bastard," Bullface growls to herself, crouching down next to Pippa's grave so no one can see. She will happily wait. Maybe that's what she should do. She thinks of the victims again, that pain that had been slashed across their skin. They didn't deserve that. Pippa didn't deserve to die. None of them deserved to die. It is her job to keep people like him off the street so why isn't she doing it? Was that not why her first husband divorced her? He blamed her for Pippa's death. A policewoman should keep the drunk drivers off the streets. She should be keeping the killers off the streets. She should be doing more to protect the living. She has to keep going now. No more drinking, no more excuses. She has to think of new ways to bait this man. He must have slipped up somewhere and he would slip up again. One more slip is all she needs. They just need a break, something to highlight that one man out of the masses. She just needs to keep looking, keep thinking.

CHAPTER FOURTEEN

A s a Happy New Year rings in, dark rumours are whispered out. Friends call to greet each other but are really just checking just in case. People are disappearing every day and the paranoia is growing. Some girls have taken to carrying razor blades, secreted in pockets. One drunken girl nearly sliced an artery as she demonstrated its power. Doors are still firmly locked and chained and locked again. New Year parties have people whispering angrily in corners about how little the police appear to be doing. No one feels safe anymore. "It's up to us to protect ourselves," so many wobbly jowls proclaim. Amateur sleuths have created elaborate theories about the significance of the date and the manner in which the women were killed; some going as far as to predict when the next attacks will occur and who is at risk. Enrolment at self-defence classes has never been higher but no one's New Year's resolution is to take up jogging or running.

He tries not to snap as his relatives yell "Happy New Year" in his ear. Tries not to punch his drunken lecherous auntie as she gives him a little pinch. He really needs to get out now, really needs to go out and do something to scare them back into misery. New year, new kills. Bigger, bolder kills.

He could wait a little while longer, has to wait a little while longer, the streets are too busy with New Year parties spilling everywhere. Too many drunks collapsing in awkward places, ready to awake at any scream. Thankfully his wife seems to trust him again. Stupid woman has probably convinced herself that he had been having an affair. He really needs to get rid of her soon. She would grow suspicious again and suspicious people snoop, don't they? Not that she would find much, he has become a master at washing those annoying blood spots out of his clothing. Everything else has been locked away safely. He has made sure the others are completely hidden. No one will find them. Even if they did, they would find nothing but torched bones.

John Roberts is not having a Happy New Year. Reporters still keep trying to get in touch; none of them are interested in hearing his side of the story or how he had been unfairly fired either. John has stopped answering the house phone. He had unplugged it but his mother found out.

"What if there was an accident, Johnny?"

How have so many people got his number? It was probably his ex-girlfriend. Fucking bitch.

His fucking mother insists on answering every call. "We have nothing to hide, Johnny." It had made him briefly laugh, listening to his mother deal with the prank callers. Briefly laugh and then cringe. Why couldn't she just say, "Sorry, you have the wrong number." She is outside now cleaning again. Last night someone papered the house with egg and toilet tissue.

"This can't go on much longer, Johnny." Want to bet,

Mother?

CHAPTER FIFTEEN

He has been out a few times since New Year, always with the same disappointing results. His new favourite spots are deserted, no females can be found wandering alone. Kim Donaghue's death so close to home had hit too hard.

It is challenging. He has less reason to be out alone as well. He has seen people surreptitiously taking photographs of anyone foolish enough to attempt jogging or running. Everyone is looking at each other's faces now. He wishes he had had the foresight to buy his wife a puppy for Christmas. Not only could he be out walking it but it would have attracted a number of women. Maybe for her birthday but then, did he really want a slobbering mutt in his house? Also, dog hairs. The police would be drooling over any dog hairs on victim's clothing and if the same dog hair would be found on more than one victim, they would start looking very closely at any male dog owners. No, no dogs. There are still other ways to pick up women, still some easy catches.

They would relax soon anyway. Their new security precautions would become suffocating. He needs them to relax soon, he is stuck otherwise. If he decides to move out of the city now (his wife keeps pointing out "cute" houses in other towns) then the next murder the police would just start by looking at residents who have moved recently. His wife would notice that too – unless he moves without her. As a stranger in a new place, people would notice him more, he would be an outsider. He wouldn't have the friends he has here. It would take ages to memorise routes in a new city, he doesn't want to waste any more time. He has this city afraid, if he left the city then all his hard work will be over. He wants to see how far he can push the people, what he can make them do.

He will never be suspected in this city, his new activities make sure of that. No fingers will be pointed at him. No bricks will ever be thrown through his window. There is only one person in this city who might suspect him – his wife! How much had she told her brother anyway? He needs to look more at getting rid of them. It can't look like a murder with those two, too much of a red flag. He has spent most of Christmas dwelling over this. A car accident or a fire would be best, but how to set one up without leaving any clues?

He is irritated. He really needs a release now, really needs just one woman to let her hair down, just one or two. He wouldn't mind two. Two would be nice actually. He needs a new place to take them. He destroyed the old place when he feared his wife ... stupid bitch would pay for that too. He had to destroy it anyway, it was too closely tied to him and people were getting closer, but now he has nowhere to work quietly. If he gets rid of his wife then maybe, maybe he can take one or two back home but somewhere more secluded is more ideal. Could he really risk looking for a place like that? What sort of explanation would he give? Maybe he could with the right explanation, but if they found anything out there, he would be the first guy they would remember. He really must be careful right now, right when he really wants to go crazy. One mistake will end everything but he never realised how addictive this is, how delicious, he never thought he would last this long or kill this many. It is beautiful how well he is doing. He is better than them he always knew that, but now he has proven himself. He is better than anyone else.

Still, tonight is a cold, dark night, no one is around. It would be perfect if he could just find someone on their own. Anyone. Does it really matter if they are female? How fun would that be? The men would be the easy pickings now, wouldn't they? They won't have their guard up, they won't be scared of a stranger. Sure it would be harder, men tend to be strong, but then isn't he stronger? He usually gets them by surprise anyway. Sure, some idiots would be eager to brand him as a fucking fag but fuck them. It would send the city spinning into crazy overload, wouldn't it? Everyone would be so fucking scared they wouldn't leave their house. It would have everyone in the city shivering and checking over their shoulder. It would send out the message that no one is safe.

He likes that idea. He needs to find someone now. His fucking wife will start worrying soon, wondering what is taking him so long and even though he has a new lie to tell her, he can't face the idea of returning home without some kind of release, of having to return home to watch another boring show whilst she gibbers about nonsense. She is only bearable now when she is afraid.

No one is out. Where the fuck is everyone? Where are the stupid ones who laugh in the face of danger? Maybe he should drop into a pub. No, that is a stupid idea. The sober ones will remember him dropping in late, only sipping a small drink. No, everyone is looking after the drunk ones making sure they get home safe. One last lap around his circuit and then he will have to go home and pound his frustrations into his wife, while thinking of his previous victims.

Happy New Year, Happy Old You! Nothing has changed, Brandi's life is still boring. Only one thing is keeping her entertained now, how can she catch a killer? How does anyone catch a killer? How do they trap him? How do they lure him out of the dark and cage him? Brandi could lure him out, couldn't she? She has studied the victims carefully, just like every other amateur detective. She has spent almost as much time as the police at memorising the victims' faces, trying to look for the link between them. He didn't have a type, she decided. There is no reason that he wouldn't pick her, despite her nose. She is better looking than some of the hookers anyway, even if she isn't as pretty as her sister. She has a chance. How to find him though? Should she go out jogging, walking or clubbing? She hates clubbing alone so that is out, she doesn't want to fight whilst all sweaty, how bad would that look? How to find a man, who is out looking for a woman though ... maybe jogging or walking out in the streets.

How will she trap him? A man strong enough to kill thirty-eight women must be very strong physically. She would have to strike first. She would have no chance if he overpowers her. Oh to live in a country where tazers and pepper spray are legal! How easy would that be? Zap, out like a light, tagged and bagged. *"Hello there, Mister Policeman, I caught your man!"* *"Oh yes, I am free for a drink later."* *"What's that, Mother? You are proud of me? Not now, Mother..."* No! it is not time to fantasise. She needs to plan. How can she bring him down? By herself? How will she know him from a random creep? She will just know, won't she? Women's intuition ... intuition that had not worked so well for those other women. Had they known? Had they even been given a chance to fight back?

But what other chance does she have? She can stay in this boring life, be subjected to those degrading calls from that woman who claims to be her mother, who claims to love her if she'd only change. Well this will be changing, won't it, Mother? Everyone loves a hero, don't they? Life will finally be exciting and fun! She will be seen on the cover of magazines, she will be interviewed and maybe even get to meet some famous celebrities. People would notice her! If she can figure out how to lure him, without getting hurt then she can catch him. No, it is too stupid, too risky... too dangerous ... but it won't be boring.

She really fucking disgusts him but he has no choice. It is her or nothing. She is nothing anyway. He has seen her before sleeping on a pile of newspapers. He will have to be careful with this one, she might have fleas.

How should he approach her? He does a little walk in a circle around her, still out of her sight. Carefully checking no one else is around. She looks like the mistrusting type; life has dealt her too many blows. She doesn't look like she will accept a good Samaritan's offer but she does look desperate. The skies are threatening snow again and she seems to be burrowing into herself for warmth. Should he risk this one? If she says no then she will probably remember his face; but then if she says no, he could just kill her anyway. The minute "No" crosses her lips, slash. It is a little open here, yes, but not as public as he has done it before. He could risk this one. This filthy creature is his. He likes the message that killing her would send. It would reinforce that no one is safe. Not the mothers, not the police, not the prostitutes, no one.

One more lap, make sure the coast is absolutely clear and then he approaches.

Her eyes track him warily.

"Give you twenty for a blow job."

Usually she would refuse and run but it is very cold. Twenty will get her somewhere to stay, a hot meal. She swallows her pride and he points to the toilet block. She reluctantly follows him and gets to her knees.

Finally a release.

She bled a lot, but it doesn't matter. It is dark and his wife won't know he is home until after he cleans up. Slipped in the mud if she asks. He will put his clothes straight into the wash, carefully applying the stain remover. He had a little longer with this one than expected and finally feels happy. He hates to lower himself like this but he has to take what he can get sometimes.

It takes a few days for this one to be found. The cold has preserved her nicely. He waits eagerly each day for the news report. He enjoys this almost as much as the killings now. Seeing the outbreak of fear and hatred is fun. Wondering what these pathetic people are going to do next is fun. He nearly reports her location himself, growing more and more impatient. A little longer, he keeps telling himself. They will find her soon.

They find her on January 12th. The cleaner had come round to clean the toilets, had waited for whoever was in the disabled toilet to come out, had knocked and called out, "Are you done yet?" They thought it was another damn homeless wreck and used the universal key to slam the door open, fully intending to teach them a lesson. The anger stuck in their throat as they inhaled the coppery decay.

Bullface arrives while officers are still photographing the scene. They have a lot to photograph. Blood has splattered and smeared all across the stall, she had been pushed back onto the toilet. Her body had slipped into an uncomfortable angle and then stiffened, slowly freezing. Rigor mortis then livor mortis, as what remained of her blood began to settle. Spinal and brain fluid had begun to leak from the orifices. Had this been the weather for bugs, she would have been crawling with them.

They photograph every splatter, every position, every angle of her broken body before they even think of moving her. Already it doesn't looking promising in terms of DNA and evidence. Maybe they would find a strand or two of clothing again but this killer goes for the cheap, mass-produced clothing. Maybe they will get lucky and find a trace of spit. This looks like a frenzied attack, he would have sweated. Maybe the cold has preserved something along with this girl.

Fletcher arrives as they are loading her up.

"She has been here for several days now. It's going to be hard to estimate a time of death because of the cold. We haven't got an ID on her yet."

"Her name is Rosie," Fletcher mumbles, "she is on file."

Bullface has never known her partner to be so solemn. She is the one with a face like a bulldog, whilst he is the sensitive but joking one. He hasn't been sleeping well, she didn't have to be a detective to see that (but then who had been sleeping well?). Fletcher is as deflated as the Christmas balloons. He does little as she orders a sweep of the area, radios the station, asks Michaels to search for information on Rosie.

Fletcher had said she had been homeless for a least a year, maybe more. She was somewhere between the ages of thirty and forty. Had been arrested for petty shoplifting but not charged. Fletcher had never noticed her dealing before or soliciting. She had laughed at him when he had offered to take her to a shelter. They found some meagre belongings close by that could be hers, she had probably been sleeping in the toilet block late at night and hiding in the bushes during the day.

Bullface looks around the woods, they have been here before with Adelina Sasha. It is possible he lives near here. Somewhere within walking distance. That could be a new start to their search, checking out any possible CCTV footage around this area, seeing if any joggers come frequently. It will take a lot of watching but it could be worth it. She would get the warrant later, get one of the juniors to start watching, warning them to pay very close attention. Yes, this could be a good direction to go in. Two bodies have been found in these woods, Shannon had been taken from the woods and yet there was no evidence of the killer's car. But then, if he is walking, how did he get Shannon away from here? Ah damn it. How close was that railway tunnel to here? Maybe he could have carried her, not many people would have been in this area at night.

She walks back to her car. Fletcher is waiting close by, mobile held tight to his ear. He hangs up without saying anything.

"Why don't we talk in here?" She motions to her car. Glumly he climbs in.

"What is going on, Fletcher?"

"I am going to quit."

Oh man the fuck up!

They have finished taking swabs and samples from Rosie. The autopsy has begun. Bruises indicate she had been pulled forcibly by her wrists. First she had been deeply stabbed in the chest area and it was unlikely she had felt the five stabs that followed. She definitely hadn't felt the number 40 being cut into her right hand. It is the deepest and most defined number he has ever cut.

"And why are you going to quit?"

Fletcher thinks about telling her about the angry looks, the feeling that everyone in the station is out to get him, that he can't face the failure anymore. Fletcher briefly thinks about slapping her for her sardonic tone but then this is Bullface, not a source of sympathy. Instead he tells her the simplest explanation.

"Claire has left me. She is pregnant and wants to be with the father."

"That's not a reason to leave." She is sorry to hear this, genuinely, despite everything but also wants to talk her partner out of making a stupid decision. Maybe it is for her own selfish reasons, there are few people left now she can trust.

"She wouldn't have been sleeping around if I wasn't working all the time."

"From what I have seen, yes she would." Bullface is never anything but blunt. Again, Fletcher feels like slapping her.

"You two were fighting long before this case. If it wasn't this case, it would be something else." Hurt silence. "You have always loved her more than she loved you."

Ouch, low blow, you bitch. He turns away, ready to get out of the car.

Bulldog knows it is time to change tactics. "It's not just Claire either. I'm not blind, I can see what's going on at the station." She is a detective after all. "You are struggling to deal with people blaming you."

He isn't going to deny it, isn't going to agree with her either. She already thought of him as a pansy.

"Yes, people are blaming us for not catching him already, because they think this shit is easy. They can blame who they like but we are not guilty. We did not kill these women; we are not guilty of their murders. We have done nothing wrong. There is nothing any other officer could have done differently."

She meets his glare again, to let him know how serious she is. "What good is quitting going to do? How is it going to help anyone? Quitting won't stop you from being a cop. Quitting won't make this be over. All quitting will mean is that we will just be one more man down." She is on a roll. She hates the tough love speech but will never hesitate to use it. "You have not done anything wrong. I have not done anything wrong. We have followed every single procedure, followed every single lead. We have done everything we can. Do you think you would still be on this case if Dalbiac and Vogel had seen you as incapable? Do you think Morkam would even be paying your wages if he didn't think you were doing a good job? Who knew Rosie's name? You did, why? Because you are good at talking to people. Good at seeing people who others don't want to see. You are good at what you do. Sherlock fucking Holmes could be on this case and he would be struggling."

"Fucking cops are shite," the male voice proclaims to murmurs of agreement. Six heads are peering at maps of the city in the Taylor's living room. Jennifer Taylor adds a new mark to where Rosie had been found.

"It's not like we are much better," Joe mutters. "I was on patrol in that area and didn't see anything. There is just too much fucking ground to cover."

"We need more people to help," Chris agrees.

"Yes because there are just so many people who would be willing to risk their lives going out at night on patrols – people who can be trusted," Jennifer snaps.

She already dislikes Chris and has her doubts about Joe. But they are friends of Robert Leona who has vouched that they will be useful, but she has her doubts.

"What did you find out about John Roberts?" Mr Taylor asks Jack, in an effort to distract his wife.

"He is nothing but a Mummy's boy. I am not even sure why the police arrested him in the first place."

"What about the Krill?"

Robert Leona has been looking into this one. Some of his fellow officers are still happy to talk to him. "The house seems to be abandoned, unless this guy has a secret entrance in and out the house. No one has seen movement inside. The last food delivery was made over a month ago. The house belongs to a K. Rill which is where the nickname Krill comes from."

Jennifer isn't convinced on this one either.

Some people aren't that bothered about Rosie's death. The homeless don't mean that much to them, it is a relief to hear that the victim hadn't been another mother. Some fill with shame when they hear how a woman has been sleeping rough in this weather, at this time of year. Some cling to the theory that the killer is growing more violent, that this victim had her arms practically torn off and that this only meant there would be more attacks. The killer has completely lost his mind now, they argue, soon it will be easy to catch him as he is going to slip up more now. They have to catch him soon otherwise these murders are going to become even more frequent, more vicious.

Other rumours have spread, victims had been found without shoes or without clothes. Some women are even using this time to rifle through their partner's possessions just to make sure. No one has found anything indicating murder, however, a divorce is now being filed on the basis of other incriminating evidence.

It isn't just Fletcher who is struggling to cope, Bullface realises as she looks around the room. The cops who had been cracking jokes when they found Fran Lizzie Taylor are stone-faced and sleepless. The room stinks of defeat. They are arguing over how much more they should be seen doing. The public are arming themselves again, and there are rumours of patrolling vigilantes. Some are arguing that the plain clothes officers need to stay a secret, that the killer is more likely to operate if he doesn't know they are out there. Some are arguing that they need to say there are plain clothes out there. Some want the officers who are running surveillance on John Roberts and the Krill recalled, as they are obviously needed elsewhere. (Fletcher feels a stab of pride at this. Finally, they realise that he was right about John Roberts.) The public need more uniformed officers on patrol. They need more officers to do these patrols. They need more money to have more officers.

Bullface ignores them all and concentrates on Chief Constable Morkam. She has a plan. A plan which will take a lot of time and money and may slightly infringe certain rights but it has been done before. To her surprise, Morkam agrees and starts the bureaucracy to implement it.

CHAPTER SIXTEEN

John Roberts used to be invisible, he didn't like being invisible. It wasn't what a Rock God like him deserved. He used to have a pathetic job where no one recognised his greatness, and a girlfriend who wasn't a supermodel. He has always wanted more. Then that bitch, that meddling bitch stuck her nose in and bang he has fame. The world is watching him now but they still don't recognise his greatness. They are mocking him, laughing at him. He is exposed and alone.

"Johnny."

She wants him to sell his house. Now she has cleaned it and repainted it and made it look nice. She thinks, despite everything eventually they will get a good price for it, after they replace the smashed window. He can stay with her until the house is sold. Then he can cut or at least wash his hair, make himself a little more presentable and start again in a new city, join a new band, get a nice new job. "Isn't that a good idea, Johnny? Just think about it, Johnny. Please."

This is his house! Why doesn't the bitch across the road have to leave? She is the one who broke in, she is the one who spread the lies. She is the one who did something wrong. Not him! He doesn't want to move. Moving would mean admitting he is scared. He isn't scared. Isn't. Maybe he had been a little scared when the brick came flying through the window, but that was understandable.

"What are you going to do if you stay here, Johnny? No one is going to hire you now."

Big deal. He doesn't want to leave until he has had revenge. He can't leave without teaching Mrs Prissy Bitch a lesson. Something to scare her away from her curtains. But what?

Then again, if he moves in with his mother and puts the house up for sale, then she would think this is over. She would let her guard down. The police would move on too, there would be no witnesses or anyone to protect her. He could get his revenge when she least expects it.

"You have made the right decision, Johnny. I am proud of you." She has never said that before. Would never say it again either.

Saturday evening sees Brandi strutting down the street, finally feeling alive. Even just being out here felt daring, felt ... sexy. She is in control, she has power. She can almost feel the eyes watching her and she shakes her butt in response. She strides, imagining herself walking down the red carpet, surrounded by adoring admirers. Her heels tap out her own personal drum roll. Her dress sashays and swishes as she moves. She turns another corner onto an empty street. She begins to imagine the television interviews she will give, they will ask her, was she scared? And she will come up with something witty that implies she is as strong as any hero. Then the handsome television presenter will laugh and give her flowers. She will appear on every television across the country, looking more beautiful than her sister.

Brandi crosses the road and walks into the park.

She walks past an *Appeal for Information* poster and then another. Looking up, she sees the posters stuck on every possible area; all blazing with Madison Albrook's picture. They didn't look that different, did they? Madison was younger of course, a lot younger. Madison has a nicer nose but otherwise, they weren't that different. Brandi could maybe have passed as her aunt.

He must have met Madison somewhere near here. Brandi had originally romanticised this. They had met in secret in the park and then gone into the bushes ... then he had cut this baby university student's throat. At the point in her life where she should have been having fun, she was dead. Brandi's eyes cross over to the flower displays; this is where Madison had died, leaving only wilted stained memorial poppies. So many strangers have come here, leaving cut flowers in her memory, most were old and rotting but there were some fresh Christmas flowers. Someone even left a cookbook and a teddy bear. A teddy bear, alone in the cold, wearing a jumper that reads *Miss You*.

The girl had died just where Brandi is standing. Brandi's heart double beats. Just right here, she could die just as fast as Madison. Just like that. Murderers come back to the scene of the crime, don't they? He could be anywhere here and she is alone. If he strikes her first then she won't have a chance, despite her preparations. What had she been thinking earlier? About being on the television, with her face plastered all over the news. She is more likely to be a victim than a hero. She really doesn't want to be a victim ... or even a hero anymore.

This is really stupid. Why is she being so stupid? She should go home now before ... is he here? Is he watching her already? Brandi feels sick, her body begins shaking. Could she even get home safe now? What if he follows her home? Oh God, what should she do?

"What are you doing out here?"

Brandi's heart rockets through her throat. She is going to die, she knows it, she is going to die here in the park because she has done something stupid. She can't even run in these stupid heels.

"Don't you know there is a killer on the loose?"

Brandi turns to see a mousey woman bearing down on her. The fear melts away and she nearly hugs the woman in relief. Should she say what she is really doing? She doesn't want to be laughed at.

"Nothing," Brandi mutters defiantly. What is this woman doing out here alone? Hypocritical woman! They square off. The mousey woman eyes Brandi's dress up and down, narrows her eyes, a lecture is being prepared. Brandi in turn is alternating between decisions. Does she stay, this woman could help protect her or does she run away from the judgement? Her mother will never stop laughing if she hears about this one.

"Jen?" A male voice pants out of sight. Brandi can hear footsteps running closer. What had the newspaper said? That there might be two of them? Her fists clench up, her homemade mace is still in her handbag. She should have taken it out ages ago. Stupid! Stupid! She has no chance if there are two of them.

"Jen?" the voice pants again.

The mousey woman stops studying Brandi and calls out, "Over here."

"Jack's gone crazy, Jen, he says he is going into the Krill's house."

Jen closes her eyes and inwardly curses. Joe finally comes into view, a red flushed face with a purple black eye. "I tried to stop him, Jen. I am sorry."

Jen had her worries about Jack but never expected him to do

anything this stupid. Damn it. She notices the panic flaring on the other woman's face and makes her decision.

"Walk this woman home, Joe," she snaps and hurries off towards her car.

"Umm. Hi." Joe murmurs bashfully. "I don't have to walk you home if you'd rather be alone ... she is a little paranoid."

"No, please, I would really like that."

Joe walks home with the satisfaction of a job well done. He texts Jennifer to let her know that the woman is home safe and he is done for the night – unless of course she needs help with Jack. He hopes everything is OK but he has to be up in a few hours for work.

Luckily his wife supports his efforts and appreciates what he is doing. He walks into the kitchen, wolfs down a ham sandwich before retiring to bed.

In bed, lying next to his sleeping wife he lies awake, contemplating his next move. Should he patrol some of the previous kill sites or should he start on new territory?

Another Sunday evening, he has lost count of the Sundays he has sat here. Officer Jayman has been watching this house for far too long. They can't get a warrant to go inside but people won't stop calling the police help line about this house. It is clearly abandoned, people! No one home! Why is he still watching it? This is such a waste of time. He should be patrolling elsewhere. Perhaps maybe elsewhere he would have a chance of helping someone. Maybe he should just go. No one would notice if he just slips off for a while, would they? Just to warm up a little.

Jayman hears the sound of a door being kicked open, a loud splinter on the quiet night. He fumbles for his radio and calls for back-up before nervously getting out of the car. What the blazes is going on?

Jack takes a deep breath and kicks as hard as he can at the rotting door. If the police aren't going to do anything about this creep then he will. The smell of damp hits his nose as the door falls open. There is no going back now.

The house is dark and musty. Jack hasn't bothered bringing a torch. He knows that splitting open the door is going to bring attention. No point creeping around like a murderer. The Krill, he has been reliably told "masturbates to your wife's picture every night." He doesn't question how they might have known that. No thinking at all. In his mind, he is going to storm this house and see the truth. All evidence will be on show for the admiring cops. He is going to pummel the bastard's head in and then this will all be over. If he can just find the bloody bastard. Jack runs up the stairs to the bedrooms. Both are completely empty, no beds, no wardrobes, just musty rooms with the wallpaper peeling. Fuck. This is supposed to be easy. He can hear the sirens blazing already. He doesn't want to run away, doesn't want to leave without finding this guy. Kitchen, empty. Living room – nothing but spiders. Wait. Back to the kitchen. What is hiding in the shadow of the refrigerator? Another door. He yanks it open. Storms down the steps, rage erupting and the police close behind.

Jack is first hit by an overwhelming stench of cigarette smoke. When his eyes focus again he can see a small makeshift bed is in one corner, a pile of clothes folded next to it. Another corner, he can see several bulk packages of cigarettes, water and pot noodles. A few jars of coffee and clang, a kettle clunks against his head as a figure whacks him onto the floor and makes for the stairs.

It was dirty cream, perhaps it once was white. Time and other activities yellowed and disfigured the once clean ceiling. In the centre was a dirty brown patch. A pulsating patch that transformed in shape and size the longer Kayla stared. To her, the patch whispered secrets that she did not wish to hear.

Some people found it peaceful to lie down and just stare. Kayla had been an active person and this was the longest she had ever been still. The dirty throbbing patch was all she could focus on. She was blinkered to it, all so her eyes didn't have to see the flakes of reddish brown splattered across the walls.

She had started talking to the patch; to it she had promised to be good from now on. She had threatened the patch and she had cried to it. She had tried to reason with the patch but despite everything, nothing. The patch was as unforgiving as the straps that bound her. She was reduced to begging. "Please let me go home... Please let me go home." A mantra on her trembling lips. "Please, please. Please let me go HOME!"

Around her the creaks began to whisper warnings as he slithers in. Slowly moving his hands across her navel, gloating over his damaged prey. His fingers move upwards, brushing away long strands of soft hair. Then he leans in, breathing noxious curry breath into her face. Panic bubbles within her as she chokes on his rancid warm breath, as he invades her skin and senses.

"I am going to make you beautiful," he murmurs tenderly before reaching for his scalpel.

The knife cuts deeply into her cheek, arching down into a cruel smile. Kayla screams as blood cascades into her mouth, a bubbling scream as the coppery blood threatens to drown her. Breath comes in gasps now, all thoughts of screaming blanketed in blood.

"Hush, let me work" he soothes, pushing her bleeding face downwards, draining her mouth again.

Kayla can't focus as the pain crackles and explodes. No! He

205

is going to do the other side! Her hands and legs have fought too hard against the straps and now are crying with their own pain. She can't breathe. He strokes her hair.

"I could take out this skin here and replace it with this ... or I could take this bit out? Which do you prefer?" A thoughtful pause. "No I think we should take this part off. You need to stop moving so much, you are putting me off," he admonishes.

That's the last thing Kayla remembers. It was the last time Kayla was really Kayla. They saved her a cut too late. After the hospital stay, after the endless investigation, the questioning, the counselling, Kayla just did not want to be Kayla any longer. Kayla was the girl who used to be pretty. Kayla was the girl who wanted to be a model. Kain is the girl who wakes up, choking on the taste of her own blood most mornings. Kain is the ugly girl, who sometimes forgets she is still a girl. Kain is the being taken away from the world and hidden safe in the cellar. Kayla Rill is the person who does not want anything anymore except to play computer games and drink coffee, alone, where no one can admire her beautiful hair or stare at the scar running down her face, a piece of Kayla that can never be hidden not matter how hard Kain tries.

The police grab her shrieking on the stairs. Kain can't comprehend where all these people have come from. Why are they in her house? Get away! Leave me alone! Why her? Why can't they leave her alone? They bundle her, still kicking, into Officer Jayman's car and drive her away into the dark.

Kayla Rill has left the house for the first time since she moved here, four years ago. Moved in and went straight to the cellar. She chose the house because it looked secure, bars covered the lower windows (not just on her house, on the whole street). Only problem was the park down the road. But out of all the houses she had seen in this new city, this one looked the safest. It may have stayed safe had she kept up on the repairs and replaced the doors, but instead she went straight downstairs and stayed downstairs. The only time she came up was for food deliveries (once every couple of months, when she couldn't hold out any longer). She never told anyone where she lived, didn't even speak to the people on her online games for fear they might ... do something.

She is driven away from her home that night and never returns.

Bullface watches through the glass as Fletcher patiently sits with Kayla. This is the longest Kayla has been without caffeine and nicotine and it is not going well. It's not going well at all. She has almost completely bitten off her nails and her hands won't stop shaking. She can barely breathe, no matter what Fletcher says. Fletcher knows this, Fletcher knows he could be talking another language and it wouldn't matter. What is needed is a soothing voice and patience. Kayla has begun to rock herself; occasionally Bullface sees flashes of that long red facial scar as Kayla's head bobs forwards and back. She sees pallid skin and dark shadows under the eyes, not too dissimilar to her own dark shadows. Kayla is going to the overpopulated observation ward; it's going to be a long time before she is released. Nothing will ever feel safe again.

Jack Sasha has been taken to hospital with a concussion. Physically, he will be fine. Bullface is waiting to hear if Kayla wants to press charges. Lawyers will be involved regardless. Bullface and Robert Leona glare at each other across the table.

"What the hell were you thinking?"

"We were just trying to do what you failed to do." An angry pause. "Go on, tell me all that crap, Shannon wouldn't want this for me. This won't bring Shannon back."

"Shannon would never forgive you if you were arrested."

"I had to do something."

"Do you really think we were just sitting around?"

"No, but it wasn't enough."

"So attacking an innocent woman, that's enough?"

"I didn't think Jack would break into her house."

"Oh, so what were you trying to do?"

"I just ... I was just trying to stop Jennifer Taylor from getting hurt. She was going to go out patrolling the streets alone. I couldn't just sit at home, knowing she was out there with no back-up. What if she had been hurt?" A deep breath. "I never thought they would do anything like this. We had agreed that the house was abandoned, that the Krill was probably just an urban legend. I never thought Jack would..."

"I think you need counselling, Robert."

"I need you to do your fucking job, Bullface, and catch this bastard." He lowers his head again. Part of him knows that a, he is being unfair and b, he is now a dead man for calling her Bullface to her face. A lump forms again in his throat. "I just want Shannon's wedding ring back."

"We have reason to believe that the killer may live in this area," Chief Constable Morkam announces, tracing an outline on the map. "We are asking all males aged between eighteen and fifty to give a DNA sample within the next twenty days."

Morkam has agreed to Bullface's plans. They have a warrant and HQ's blessing. There will be outrage but Morkam is willing to tackle it. They will announce that these samples will not be kept on file, not be used to prosecute other non-violent cases, just to ease the uproar. There will still be refusers. They are going to be very interested in the refusers. It will overload an already overworked lab but it will be worth it. It will mean narrowing an area of five hundred potential suspects to hopefully no more than a handful. Maybe also now that they are seen to be doing something, the public might trust them again. Maybe this will stop any other outsiders from being targeted. They hope.

"They can't arrest us for walking around in the streets. We can't let this stop us," Jennifer says.

"They can arrest us for disturbing the peace."

"Until they impose a curfew, I am staying out."

"I am not joining you." Robert Leona's voice is final against his friends' perhaps a private chat with Bullface did some good after all. Chris and Joe stare at him in disappointment; Jennifer studies her coffee cup. Robert stands up. "You people are bloody idiots if you keep doing this." He slams out of the door.

"He is just upset, he will come round," Chris mutters unconvincingly.

Jennifer says nothing.

"Maybe we should stop, the four of us aren't going to be that effective."

"For fuck's sake, Joe!" Chris looks around for someone else's support.

Mr Taylor waits on his wife's lead. Nothing. "Let's take a break, see if Robert comes to his senses," Mr Taylor finally says. "We won't patrol tonight and we will talk again tomorrow." Another person slams out. Mr Taylor nods at Joe awkwardly before also retreating.

"Are you OK, Jen?"

"That poor woman."

"We weren't to know, Jen. If it hadn't been Jack, it would have been someone else. So many people have talked about it."

Jennifer's eyes focus on her daughter's photograph. All that planning, all that preparation, for what? Another woman has died, a homeless woman and what did they do to help? They targeted a completely innocent woman. A vulnerable woman.

"Why don't you get some sleep, Jen?"

She isn't listening, too many people have told her to get some sleep recently. "I think I might have another lead, why don't we meet tomorrow and talk about it?"

CHAPTER SEVENTEEN

"*H*ello, Brandi! Guess what? Your sister has got engaged! Isn't that wonderful? She wants you to be in charge of the guest book! It would be a perfect opportunity for you to get to know Brian. Give me a call back and we will talk about your dress.*"

She scratches him with something sharp. He hadn't expected that. Bitch must have had it in her hand the entire time. He can feel warm blood trickling down his face. Oh it is on, bitch! She goes for another strike. He slashes at the offending arm with his knife. Whatever she has scratched him with, clatters onto the floor. She screams and rakes her other hand across his face, plunging sharp nails into his cheek. With a furious shove, he plunges his knife deep into her chest. Game over, bitch. She splutters and stops, fuck, he didn't mean to kill this one so quickly. He intended to make the bitch bleed more for scratching his face. What the fuck had she struck him with? Where did it go? His fucking blood is going everywhere.

He reaches to pull his knife out of her chest, time to brand this bitch. Behind him, he hears the sound of someone running. He looks up to see a figure about a hundred metres away and closing. He stands, turns and runs.

"Stop!"

No fucking way. He keeps running down an alley and out of sight. Bleeding all the way.

"Brandi! Darling, why haven't you called me back yet? I know you are busy but please call me back."

Fletcher reaches the girl and is about to keep chasing the suspect, when he hears her give a weak splutter. She is alive ... he can't leave her.

"I need an ambulance now," Fletcher screams into his radio, reeling off his location and the direction the suspect ran. The girl splutters again, knife still lodged deep within her chest. Helplessness washes over Fletcher. There is nothing he can do to save her ... and he has let the suspect go.

She is dead by the time the ambulance arrives. But there is still hope. In her nails, there is the killer's DNA, ready to be clipped and placed in paper packets and tamper-proof sealed bags. The knife is carefully removed and sealed. The dropped razor blade photographed, bagged and sealed; the blood drops swabbed and sealed. Irrefutable evidence if they catch him.

It is a pity Fletcher only really saw his back, not enough to identify him. It is a shame the pursuing officers don't know that the killer is bleeding, don't know that a very small blood trail is being left. Very small spots, splattering every other step. But they have his blood.

It is enough to ease some of the tension back at the station. Out of their list of five hundred names, they have already received a hundred grudgingly given DNA samples. Now they are sure that they had the killer's DNA from the razorblade. If Bullface is right, their list of suspects is about to get a lot smaller. If Bullface is right! Some have their doubts, they believe her theory is flimsy but even they can't deny that they are getting closer. They still have the girl to identify though, it is too early for her to be reported missing and she doesn't appear to be carrying a purse.

Fletcher still quits, that last splutter still replaying in his mind. Enough is enough.

"Hi, Brandi, this is Mike. Just wondering why you weren't at work today. Please give me a call back soon. Hope you are OK."

Elizabeth Mitchell sips her tea slowly. Finally she feels at peace. Old Arnie's place has gone up for sale. The hooligan is gone. She saw him and his mother loading up the small moving van. The skip filled with his rotting nasties has been taken away. The house looks nice and welcoming again. She is sure he was glaring at her when his mother wasn't looking. He was harmless she can see that now, harmless and pathetic. Elizabeth Mitchell hopes whoever buys the house, buys it soon, she doesn't want the boy to change his mind and come back. Definitely does not want him to even think about coming back.

Elizabeth closes her eyes; she hasn't slept well in weeks. She thought he would do something. She has been waiting and watching for something. Always in reach of the phone, ready to call the police if he should even dare come on to her property.

The doorbell rings interrupting her peaceful afternoon.

"Brandi, please call Mother, she is really upset that you haven't called her back yet. Please don't be upset that I am getting married before you."

It is over now. He really fucked that one up. Had Fletcher seen him? Had that even been Fletcher? It sounded like him … Fletcher probably hadn't seen him, he made sure to keep his head down and run without looking back … had it been anyone else then they wouldn't have recognised him. But they were going to recognise him now, weren't they? Even the people who hadn't noticed him before, everyone was going to notice him. What had that fucking bitch cut him with? What had she done to his face? He needs to get home. Needs to see what she has done. Fuck. Fuck. Fuck. Is anyone still following him? Has anyone else seen his bleeding face? The darkness seems to be working in his favour, but he isn't sure. Everything is going wrong tonight.

Home.

Bathroom.

He surveys the damage to his face. It isn't bleeding as badly as he thought, finally a little luck. There is no way he would have been able to go to hospital for stitches. He could have told them his best lie but they would have still been suspicious. The nail gouges could have come from only one thing. He held one of the best white towels against the deep razor cut. There is no hiding this one, it runs straight across his other cheek. No one would believe a shaving accident. No one would believe a cat attack. It doesn't really matter anyway. It was going to be over sooner or later, he knew that, just wished he had more time. He carefully applies a large plaster to the nail marks. A plaster will make it easier to explain. Back to the long razor line, it has stopped bleeding, that's good, but it is too long for any kind of plaster. Anger wells inside, he really hopes that fucking bitch has died.

It was the news report earlier that had set him off, set him out hunting. The report said, "This is the area where he lives." His name is probably already on the list of suspects. How the fuck had they figured out where he lived? Had someone seen him? Did they already know? No, if someone had seen him, he would have been arrested already. The DNA request had been slipped through his door while he was out. But they are testing hundreds of men, he had a little more time. But time to do what? If he refuses to take the test, it is a massive bullseye. If he asks someone to go in his place, well that will work only if there is someone stupid enough to take the test for him and loyal enough not to blabber. No, anyone he asks is likely to go running straight to the police. What had the request said? Within twenty days. After tonight, it will be nineteen, at least. Depends on how long it takes to go through the results. That was enough time to go down with a bang, wasn't it? That's what sent him out hunting with a careless fury.

His face really fucking hurts. He knew she would be trouble when he first saw her. That's why he chose her. She looked like a challenge. A dark-haired girl with an even darker scowl. Everything about her screamed misunderstood youth, leave well alone. She had glared at him. "What the fuck do you want?" Since no one had been around, he didn't even bother trying the nice guy routine. But when he had tried to grab her, she slashed at him with something sharp. Bitch must have had it in her hand the entire time, just waiting for someone to fuck with her. Just like he had his knife in his hand the entire time, half hidden up his sleeve so no one could see – waiting for someone.

"Brandi, if you don't call Mother back soon, then you are not going to be in my wedding at all!"

He has been working so hard for years for this. So many years exploiting the city's weak spots. Looking for dump sites, the places where not so many people dare go. Studying endless forensic and true crime magazines so every rookie mistake could be avoided. So much time spent being perfect. OK, maybe his first ones weren't perfect but it's not like anyone noticed. So much time in proving he was better than everyone else. So much time enjoying himself. He always knew he would enjoy this, even as a child, he just enjoyed hurting people. His mother thought he had grown out of it. He just became better at hiding the evidence, convincing other children it was in their best interest not to say anything. He has always known he was better than these people, that they were his to control and destroy. It had all been so perfect.

Even his job was perfect, factory work with six days on night shift and then four days off. His wife could barely keep track of him, she knew how he loved his running, football, jogging and of course his drinking to keep up appearances. Had she suspected anything since he started? He really, really doubted it. Maybe recently, but probably not. Did he ever even love her? Well isn't that why he made that first one, that cheap little woman, number two? His wife would always be number one. He had been thinking about it for so long, fantasising over and over again about what it would be like to take a life. Masturbating over images of other people's victims, wanting his own, looking for an opportunity to lure one of the stupid ones over, without anyone seeing. Wanted so badly to feel a person's pulse fade through his fingers. Then finally he noticed her, a little no one, no one would miss her and no one did miss her. So many years on, even when he had flung them a clue, even when her reconstructed face was everywhere, no one knew as much as her name. 2 – Marie, then number 4, Amie or Abbie, something like that. Why no number three? He always knew that they would find his discarded trash one day. Never knew how far this might go but always thought they would find some. So why not fuck with them? All the even numbers, nothing odd about that, hah! There was six months between Marie and Andy, he had been so sure they would find something. He had been so sloppy, so eager with that first one he had enjoyed himself so much. Then the realisation hit, no one was watching. No one cared about these women. Why would they? Plenty of them. No one even noticed they were missing. Still kept it under control though. Had to stop for six months after his wife had broken her wrist, six irritating months he needed to be there for her, needed to keep up the good husband appearance. Then number six, another hooker, one with a funny name, Flonna or Flora. Then there had been that teacher, Joanna. He had been really surprised no one had noticed her sooner. She had taken a lot of talking. It's when he realised he could still put on the charm, that women still liked his face. He had been doing so well. It was all coming together. No one suspected a thing and that was fine. Fine for over two years, six more secrets. Bodies were beginning to pile up and smell. He never realised how much blood and other vile things humans had, how much they could smell. Humans are really disgusting inside and out, except for him.

No one had noticed they were missing. That had been fine for a while, it meant he could snatch women away and no one would care. But then it became less fun, he wanted more, he wanted people to notice now, notice his work. He wanted them to see him, to fear him. He wanted them to know he was better than them, smarter. He saw their fear, how stupid they became when they were scared, he saw how to control them, to destroy them.

Elizabeth sits in her chair frozen. The doorbell rings again, even the once-loved melodic chimes sound threatening. Go away, go away, go away. Elizabeth tries to tell herself it is just a doorbell. Someone nice is at the door, she should get up and open it. She isn't expecting anyone but it could be her neighbour, it could be a delivery, it could be her friend Lorna ... it could be a greasy, angry hooligan. No, she can't open it. It is him, isn't it? She thought she was safe but she isn't safe, is she? Could he see her from where she was sitting? Does he know she is in here? What if he comes to the windows? No, no one could see her from this position, unless they go into the garden ... is the kitchen window still open? Someone as skinny as him could probably squeeze through if it is open...

They had been neighbours for a long time. He could have been watching her. He would know how often she was alone in the house. He would know the best way into the house. He might have even seen where the spare key was kept ... what was that thought she had earlier? He was harmless. Harmless and pathetic. Was he really though? She remembers the look of pure hatred he had given her when he was leaving. She had thought he was responsible for the deaths of those poor girls. She had almost been certain of it, especially when she went into his room and saw those awful satanic posters. Then to see that poor girl's wallet ... she was only trying to protect them. He wouldn't see it like that, would he? He would be back for revenge. She would have to be ready for him, ready for when he came back. She has to get up and protect herself. She has to get up. She has to get up.

Then when they knew about him, when they were shitting themselves trying to work out his numbers, he had to do bigger, better more daring ones. He was still proud of luring away the cop, Shannon. She knew him vaguely, had been talking quite happily to him as they searched. Not even questioning why he was there, just thinking he was a volunteer. He'd had to be careful about keeping out of sight of the others, so no one would inconveniently remember seeing him. They were so close to searching near his place, he had been worried that they were going to find it, but then the sun started going down. She had bent down to tie her shoe and head met rock, cop shock.

He had burnt his place after her, just in case they decided to search again. He really missed that place, it was so beautifully hidden and there were plenty of areas in that wood for disposing of the decomposing. But he had to burn it, it was too risky now if anyone went for a second look in the woods.

"Her name is Ebony Jackson. She was seventeen. She has a record for assault and is currently suspended from school. It is too early to say if this is the same suspect as our serial killer as there was no number on her hand."

Bullface is feeling a little nervous. Had this kill been prompted by their news announcement? Is it confirmation that they had picked the right area? Did a girl die today because of her? No, she has to focus. If this was an attack because of the announcement then the killer must know he is running out of time. They need to be out there, before he picks another girl. They need to be ready.

He just can't see how they had figured out his home area. Where has he slipped up? What gave him away? He doesn't want to stop now. He is enjoying himself so much. He has seen how crazy the city is becoming, how paranoid and he wants to see how far he can push them. Just how stupid and reckless they can be. There is still time to do that. They haven't found him yet and until his face is blasted on every television in the city, he has time, plenty of time to make an impact. To prove he is still better than them.

The house will have to go now, there is too much evidence secreted away inside. Then there is the little matter of his wife. She has been sleeping peacefully upstairs since he heard the DNA announcement. Soon, people will notice she is missing. Where is he to hide now? People will take one look at his face and start asking questions. If he hides out in this house for a little while longer, he will be trapped. It is best to disappear and then decide on a next move. Just in case people are watching his house, like he has been watching theirs.

He packs a rucksack, a spare change of clothes, some more nice sharp toys, as much food as he can carry and then his tent and sleeping bag. Not forgetting some antiseptic and plasters, no guessing what that skank might have had in her nails. Ready to go out into the cold.

How is best to do this? Should he pour accelerant? The police will start looking for him if they suspect arson. A burnt house, dead wife and missing husband? Wasn't going to take a genius on this one, but then if he tried to make it look like an accident, he would risk certain things like his bloody but bleached clothes being found. He doesn't want to destroy his souvenirs either. Could he risk carrying the camera and his keepsakes? Should he bury them somewhere safe? A freshly dug patch in the garden wasn't going to arouse any suspicion, was it? They are going to suspect him sooner or later anyway, why not just spell it out to these idiots exactly what he has done, how great he was? Start a fire but leave his photos out in a safe place.

They are going to suspect him as soon as they find Brandi anyway. He had to kill her, bitch had mumbled on the way home about how she had changed her mind and she was so scared. She had told him her whole plan about how she wanted to capture him and be a hero. He thought he was pushing his luck killing her but just couldn't resist such an easy kill. She had practically given herself to him. He thought by the time her body was found, no one would know exactly how long she had been dead ... well, if Jennifer Taylor puts two and two together they will suspect him. He would have got away with it for a long time, had they not guessed his area. Even if they had brought him in for questioning as a witness, one DNA swab as a precaution – damn. As a witness he will say he walked her home and left her there, but thought she was going to go back out again. He will say that when he walked her home, she had talked about how determined she was to be the hero. Say she had been alive and looking to go back out again. He could get away with that, until they noticed his home address and asked for a DNA sample, just to be sure. He could talk his way out of a lot of things but not DNA evidence.

Would the others suspect him when they heard about Brandi? No one had seen him with her except Jennifer, briefly. Maybe Jennifer wouldn't remember because of Jack. She might have been too distracted and distraught to remember sending him home with her. He thought Jack suspected him a little, he thought Jack would be fun to play with as well. He had all these plans about sending him photos of Adelina, just to see what would happen. Jack was easy to push, easy to manipulate. It took one little whisper, one little rumour and boom, Jack was running after the Krill. It had just been so easy. He would have loved to see Jack's reaction when he found out he had happily patrolled alongside the man who had killed his wife. Robbie's and Jennifer's reaction as well. This would crush them. Crush them completely. He had planned to meet Jennifer tomorrow but it was too risky now. Had planned to have so much fun with her. Maybe he should still make that meeting but, as soon as she saw his face, she would start asking questions. What to do, what to do, what to do?

Stay here for one more night, he decides, no one suspects him yet. He can have a good night's sleep. See how bad his face looks in the morning.

CHAPTER EIGHTEEN

Joe wakes up feeling refreshed. Last night he had been too paranoid. Too much reminiscing about the good times, he needs to plan now. Think carefully. He wishes he knew how much the police knew. How much evidence did they really have? They have one of his knives, he knows that much. They have his DNA, yes, but not anything to match it against. Nothing in their records would say this DNA belongs to Joe. They have a start but they still don't know who they are looking for. They don't have as much as a name or a face.

What had he been about to do last night? Burn down his house – a big glaring beacon in the darkness, screaming investigate me, investigate me! That was a smart idea, wasn't it? No, they hadn't found that Brandi girl yet, it could take them a while to find her, it might take them a while to find his wife as well. Just leave her upstairs in the bedroom and lock the doors. Maybe they will even think it was someone else who attacked her, for a while. If they found her a lot later, then she might be too decomposed for them to figure out what really happened. He could say they had a fight and he left her. Left her alive. Challenge them to prove otherwise. He still had a while before the DNA deadline, over two weeks. Maybe no one will look in his house until then. Depends how worried they got at her work. How long it took to notice they were missing. It wasn't safe to stay in the house much longer, but they hadn't found him yet.

What options did he have?

He could go and live in John Roberts' house. He knows it is empty now, who would think to look there? But then, there was a nosey busybody living opposite, she would notice if someone moved in across the road. She would be watching. He could kill her and they would probably blame that kid. But then if the house is still under surveillance or if they look in the house for evidence then it's game over.

Either he ends it now (the pussy way out), sets fire to the house and stays inside. Or he kills as many people as he can, before they catch him or he moves to another city and starts again, moving from city to city. Decisions, decisions, decisions.

When Mr Mitchell comes home, he finds a *Sorry to have missed you* notice at his feet, along with a small pile of post. Elizabeth didn't say she was going anywhere. The answerphone has four new messages. He walks into the kitchen, to check if she has left him a note and finds her still sitting in the corner. Where he had left her this morning, breakfast plate and teacup still in front of her. Mr Mitchell is astounded to see his normally rational, steel-nerved wife shaking. By Tuesday morning he puts the house up for sale and starts to move their belongings into storage. He is determined his wife will not live the rest of her life in fear.

John Roberts never gets his revenge; he fantasises about it a thousand times but just never quite gets round to it.

He has lit the flame. It is time to add the kindling. The best place to start would be with her. That woman he has always hated, from the moment he met her. Hated her stern face, hated her for looking like his mother, hated her monotone voice, hated everything about her! Yes, the best time to get her is now, before they know who he is. Get in the first strike.

He needs to think this through carefully. How will he lure her? She has never been one for charms and compliments. Also he needs to plan for after her, when she is dead he needs to have the next move ready. Hit them as fast and as frequently as he can.

"Hey, Jen, sorry, lead was no good. Not going to be able to meet today. Wife sick. Hope you OK."

Brandi Parr was a fan of floral wallpaper and lace, Bullface notes, the garish colours are making her feel a little nauseated. A few days of decomposition and dried blood spatters don't faze her anymore but bad decorating does.

"We received a call earlier. Apparently one of her neighbours noticed the smell. Not sure which neighbour but I have got four officers going around, interviewing them. She has been dead between three and five days."

She had been beaten badly, worse than Adelina and Shannon. The splatters and the bloody gag indicate that, for the first time he had attacked someone in their own home. This one had died before Ebony Jackson, they were certain of that. Brandi had the number 42 cut deep into her left hand, almost cut to the bone like Rosie's number 40 had been. They had missed 41 somewhere and Ebony would have been 43 ... or higher.

There is nothing left for her to do here. The investigators will take a long time going over the rooms, so much to dust and photograph. Only thing Bullface can do is talk to Brandi's family.

She leaves the apartment. Outside, the chill winter air feels refreshing, she takes a deep breath before unlocking her car and climbing in. As she reaches for the seatbelt, the rear passenger door quickly opens and closes. Before she can react, a sharp blade is pushed against her throat.

"Drive, bitch."

Obediently she starts the engine.

"Bet you can guess who I am." She looks in her rear-view mirror, recognising Joe immediately.

"I called in this one in, I knew you would come. I have been waiting for you," he boasts. "You know the way to the woods by now, don't you?" He has big plans. Once he has done with her, he will use her phone to lure Fletcher to the woods. Then maybe Jennifer or Robbie or both, probably both. He is still better than them, he can take them all, one person at a time. Maybe he will kill the entire city before moving on. Maybe he can evade them forever. He is smart, he knows how to stay ahead. He can change his name. His face will heal. He can still be the greatest serial killer ever.

Bullface thinks about how badly Brandi had been brutalised and accelerates a little. Not enough for him to notice.

"So, Bullface." He adores using that hated nickname. No answer. No matter. He will make her talk soon enough. Make her scream and beg.

Victoria Bullrush has seen enough victims to know what he is going to do to her. Going to the woods will mean enduring the same torture as Shannon Leona. She can't see a way out of this, it either ends here or it ends there. The minute she stops the car then it is over. She isn't a fool. He has a knife, strength and the upper hand. She has the steering wheel. She thinks of Fletcher blaming himself for letting the killer go. This man has been his friend, had been one of his groomsmen. He had been Robbie's friend too. He had taken everything, the lives of so many women, innocent women. She has to do something. She cannot bear to see anyone else die now. There is only one other thing she can do.

Had he really thought that she was a coward? That she isn't afraid to do something reckless, knowing she is going to die either way? Had he really thought she would be afraid? She accelerates, pushing the car to its limits as he makes empty threats from the back seat. Seatbelt still unbuckled. Her last thoughts are of Pippa as the car hits the wall.

It is her job to keep the criminals off the street – one way or another.

IN MEMORIAM

1. Wife
2. Marie Eine
4. Abbie
6. Flora Brittany
8. Joanna Reagan
10. Selena Alberta
12. Evie
14. India Corey
16. Verity Hayley
18. Eloise Rio
20. Jennifer Eden
22 Fran Lizzie Taylor
24. Siobhan Melody
26. Adelina Sasha
28. Stella McQam
30. Shannon Leona
32. Roxanne
34. Isobel Hilarie
36. Madison Allbrook

38. Kim Donaghue
40. Rosie
42. Brandi Parr
44. Ebony Jackson

Victoria Bullrush

EPILOGUE

Anita Gardner is sixteen years old and she is no longer afraid. If you remind her now about her trip in the forest, she will laugh at her childish ways, still blissfully unaware of how close she came to victim number 8. She is all grown up and now she knows what a nerd that Mary Taylor is and spends her time mocking her and hopes that this will make the big boys finally notice her.

Anita Gardner doesn't quite look sixteen, she is at that age where she is trying so desperately hard to look older. Some would say seventeen, eighteen. He thinks nineteen but then he has never been that good at telling.

He says, "Hi" and suggests he buy her a drink. She is very pleased; she is dying to get her nails into some alcohol. He walks her swaying body home, the long way through the forest. As she trips on a branch, ripping her skirt slightly, she begins to remember her childhood fears and the bad things that hide in the dark ... a little too late.

THE END

A NOTE FROM THE PUBLISHER

Thank you for reading this book. If you enjoyed it please do consider leaving a review on Amazon to help others find it too.

We hate typos. All of our books have been rigorously edited and proofread, but sometimes mistakes do slip through. If you have spotted a typo, please do let us know and we can get it amended within hours.

info@bloodhoundbooks.com

Printed in Great Britain
by Amazon